THE FOOTHILLS OF FEAR

The Foothills of Fear

John Creasey

A SIGNET BOOK from
NEW AMERICAN LIBRARY
TIMES MIRROR

Published by
THE NEW AMERICAN LIBRARY
OF CANADA LIMITED

SIGNET TRADEMARK REG. U.S. PAT. OFF. AND FOREIGN COUNTRIES
REGISTERED TRADEMARK — MARCA REGISTRADA
HECHO EN WINNIPEG, CANADA

SIGNET, SIGNET CLASSICS, MENTOR, PLUME AND
MERIDIAN BOOKS are published in Canada by The New
American Library of Canada Limited, Scarborough, Ontario

PRINTED IN CANADA
COVER PRINTED IN U.S.A.

Part I

WHO IS SIMON COLL?

Chapter 1

THE COLL

Simon Coll turned away from the grave, and walked, white-faced, towards the lych-gate which led into the churchyard. The fourteen people who had also attended the funeral of Martha Tenby had broken up into little groups, some still in the churchyard, some already walking along the narrow road which led to the village, to Martha's cottage, to sandwiches, cakes and tea—and for the privileged four or five, a glass of sherry or port.

Among them would be Pengelly, the vicar, Esmond the church warden, the two Fraills, husband and wife, and Lockyer, the schoolmaster. They were waiting to tell him how sorry they were, how grieved; they would urge him to square his shoulders and face the future with a stiff upper lip. They were kind and friendly, and they meant so well. One part of his mind would want to thank them, and the other half would want to scream out the question which had nagged his mind for the last few months:

"*Why won't you tell me who I am?*"

All five of them watched as he approached, and he judged that they were a little uncertain of his mood. Beyond them, standing alone by the centuries-old yew tree was Dorothy Lamb, the youngest of the mourners, her years even less than his own twenty-four.

The glancing sun showed up the gold in her hair, the rich beauty of her skin, as she waited for him. In the whole of Dern Abbas this girl was probably the only one to guess the turmoil of his thoughts, unknowing that it was she herself who had first put that question into his mind.

"*Why don't you tell me who I am?*"

He drew close to the five chief mourners.

"My boy——" began Pengelly, but broke off at a nearer view of Simon's tense expression.

"Simon, my dear," said little old Ethel Fraill courageously, "it won't help if you fret too much."

Simon said: "I'm sorry. I can't come." Blindly he moved towards the old yew tree, passing Dorothy with a muttered: "I'll see you later."

By the distress in her face he could see she had hoped to comfort him; but there was no comfort for him here. Even when he should have been mourning the dead, he was asking himself that searing question:

"Why don't they tell me who I am?"

He strode on, past the ancient yew, for perhaps half a mile. There was a stile leading across the fields and up the hills. Simon followed the path, trodden smooth over the years but never greatly used. Reaching the top of the first hill, he stood still.

It was from here that he had first seen the Coll.

It was here the question had first come into the open. He had asked it before, but with no depth of feeling; not until five months ago had the importance of it come to him, striking savagely. And Dorothy, who loved him, had caused the hurt. They had walked together since, visited the pictures in Weymouth, and even cavorted at the village dance, but some barrier had come between them.

From where he stood, he could only just make out the Coll. A haze hid the blue sea beyond it, although at one point the sun broke through, striking the water with rods of fire. The Dorset coast would never look lovelier than it did today, nor the countryside more lush or richly green.

Dorothy's voice sounded again in his ear, as if the words once uttered were stamped on the air for ever.

"Isn't it funny, Si?—your name's Coll, and that cliff is called the Coll."

"Funny——" he had echoed.

But he couldn't blame Dorothy; he couldn't blame anyone. She was 'new' to the village. Her parents had bought the village shop ten years before, when she had still been a plump ten-year-old, open-faced and ever-willing to run errands, and stand chatting at Martha Tenby's back door. Five years later her father had died, leaving the running of the business to her and her mother. Mrs. Lamb had never made any secret of the fact that she hoped that Dorothy and Simon would marry. The shop would be the better for a man to run it, and Simon could never be more than odd job man at Marven Farm.

After Dorothy's carefree: "Isn't it funny, Si?—your name's

Coll and that cliff is called the Coll"—he had asked the vicar, the Fraills, Esmond and Lockyer if they could explain that coincidence. They had all said they had no idea. As far as they knew, they said, he had been the child of a married sister of his aunt's, who had died early.

That was also the story that Aunt Martha had told him, the story he had believed on the surface of his mind but doubted deep inside him.

Dorothy's words had stirred these doubts afresh, but it had been too late to ask Aunt Martha; the woman whose voice, so deep and strong and filled with laughter, had been silenced by the disaster which eventually killed her. Now he strode first down the gentle slope and then up a steeper, rougher ascent, until at last he was at the foot of the Coll itself. Near the top it was harder going, but the grass grew thick almost to the crest of the landward side. When he reached the very top, the Coll was sheer, as if some giant knife had sliced downwards, tumbling red rocks and red earth into the sea, leaving an ugly, scowling, overhanging cliff, like the mouth of hell in shadow. It was the highest point on the coast, and seemed to be apart from the rest of the coastline, for it jutted right out into the sea. On either side, lower, humbler cliffs fell into sandy inlets, whereas below the Coll the sea loomed dark and violent.

Was his answer here?

Simon looked seawards again, and Aunt Martha's voice sounded in his ears as deep and firm as ever; he could picture her strong brown hand as she pointed towards the horizon and talked of the New World there. She had talked with fondness, for although she had never set foot outside her own country, she had read a great deal about the rest of the world, and Simon had always thought—perhaps imagined—that she felt a greater warmth for America than elsewhere.

He heard a sound; the muffled beat of a two-stroke engine; not far away was a narrow road which motor cycles and even small cars could use, for the Coll was seldom free from visitors for long. Simon, still in no mood to meet his fellow-men, turned away. Stepping among the tall rocks, where it was easy to remain unseen, he looked towards the spot where the motor cycle would come in sight.

The moment he saw the red car, he knew that it was Dorothy's. She had guessed where he had come, gone back for the three-wheeled car she used for making the shop's deliveries, and had driven up to fetch him. Now he was in a dilemma. He could not

7

walk off without being seen; on the other hand, if he remained hidden she would wait until he appeared. He watched her as she swung the little vehicle round in a half circle, and got out. The wind, quite stiff now, had begun to whip the sea below into sharp, slapping waves. She stood as if challenging the weather, and Simon had a strange feeling, that there was a new, urgent quality about her.

"Siiiiii-monnnnnnnn!"

She could not be aware of his presence, yet had she wanted to draw his gaze, she could not have found a surer way. She raised her head, and held her arms behind her, at one with the cliff, the wind, the sharp urgent sound of the sea.

Simon moved out of his hiding place, and stepped towards her. If he made any sound, she did not appear to hear. As he drew closer, he was aware of the sensuous clamour of her body. She did not speak or glance at him, and now the grass muffled all sound of his approach. When he was only ten yards away from her, he knew that she realised he was there, and he wondered fleetingly whether she had seen him from the beginning and never doubted that he would come.

He knew exactly what she wanted him to do. The life-force in her was stronger than her personality or his. This was no time to think, or reason, for calculation or hesitation. Behind him was the tension of the past months and the long drawn-out crisis of the past days. Tearing at him were his uncertainties and doubts, his grief and distress—and, since he had seen the coffin lowered and the earth showered upon it, a hard, harsh loneliness.

He was almost by Dorothy's side when she turned her head.

"Hallo, Si," she said. "I thought I'd find you here."

He didn't speak, but stepping behind her, pressed her against him; he felt her yielding, and knew for sure that this was what she wanted, that it seemed as natural to her as it did to him. So they stood until she twisted round in his arms and drew his head down to hers. Then, as one, they moved towards the broken red rocks and the dark caves, where the earth would be their bed and the darkness their benediction.

*   *   *

"Si," whispered Dorothy.

"Yes, my sweet."

"Si, it's always going to be like this," she promised. "You'll soon forget how unhappy you've been. I know, I know."

8

"Yes," he said. "Of course."

Her body was warm, too warm, now that the first exciting coolness of touch had gone. When she said, "It's always going to be like this," he felt an involuntary shudder, a clamouring protest.

Soon, Dorothy said:

"I think we ought to be going, dear. I'll drive you down to the village."

I'll look after you, she was really saying, and she meant that. But she did not know the answer to the question which obsessed him.

Who am I?

The sun's rays caught the high crimson crest of the Coll as they started away from the sanctuary of the cave, and cast a dark shadow on and beyond them. Simon shivered. Dorothy's fingers were tight about his, and still warm. There was an abandon about her which he had never known before, and a deep sense of satisfaction, almost of triumph. She knew exactly what she wanted, and believed that she had made quite sure of it. For him it was otherwise. He tried not to see her broad possessive smile as he sat by her side, the small three-wheeler forcing thighs and legs in too-close unity.

It was thus they drove away from the brooding Coll.

Chapter 2

QUESTION . . .

"All I want to know," Simon said, "is who I am."

"My boy, all I know is what your aunt told me, and I've every reason to believe that it's true," said Mr. Pengelly. His collar encircled too loosely his puckered neck; he eased it away. "After all, you've had a very happy life, you've been well cared for, and I must say that everyone who knows you is most happy about the result. Your Aunt Martha was always very proud of you, indeed we all are. We hope that when you and——" he broke off, then started again. "We hope that when you've settled down with a wife you'll be very happy, and one of the pillars of the village. The village life of the country is the country's heart, you know— its heart, and sometimes I think its soul as well. Now I suggest . . ."

Dark, squat, grey Esmond, the church warden, was a comparative newcomer, and there was no reason to believe that he would know more than the vicar. The headmaster at the school, which served not only this village but a scattering of others, had been here for just seven years. Only the Fraills were likely to know the truth.

"Simon my boy," said old Ben Fraill, "Martha Tenby was the most truthful woman, the most honest woman I've ever known. You can safely believe her. Now, I would like to suggest . . ."

After ten minutes, Simon said brusquely:

"Mr. Fraill, will you answer me one question?"

"Well, yes, of course, my boy." Fraill's eyes looked steadily at him out of a pink, healthy face. He owned the three thousand acre Marven Farm, the biggest in the district; and he had been saying that he could not expect to continue in active management of it much longer. His two sons would inherit it, of course, but they would not be able to run the farm alone; Simon could be quite sure of a secure future. "What question do you want me to answer?"

"Mr. Fraill," Simon asked, "am I Martha Tenby's illegitimate son?"

He had never seen Fraill so startled; and he felt quite sure that the old man was taken too much by surprise to lie.

"Good gracious, no!" he exclaimed. "Whatever put that notion into your head? You can put it right out, anyhow—God bless my soul, Martha Tenby——" He actually laughed. "I wish she were here to answer that question, she'd give you plenty to think about! Now, I was saying: you can rely on a job here, or on all the business that the farm can give you if you marry into the village shop, so to speak—we can talk frankly, my boy, can't we? I'm sure that would be a good thing. Now, I suggest——"

He broke off, as Simon stood up.

"Are you feeling all right, my boy?"

"No," Simon said thickly. "No, I'm sorry. I've a splitting headache." He moved towards the door. "And I have to go into Weymouth this evening. Mr. Lessinger is staying late at his office to see me. Thank you for your advice, sir. Goodnight."

He went out, knowing that Fraill was staring unhappily at the closed door, guessing that the old man came to the window to watch him. He walked briskly along the road leading to the village. He could see the church tower, the avenue of beeches, and the swinging sign outside the shop. It was after five-thirty and the shop would be closed. Dorothy was going to drive him into Weymouth to see Lessinger, his aunt's solicitor, about the will.

There had been some delay, but when it had been read no one had been surprised that everything she possessed had been left to Simon. He did not know whether it was likely to be fifty pounds or five hundred. Money and Aunt Martha had never gone together—she had had a pension, a cottage rent-free for life, and needed, or wanted, nothing more. He wasn't thinking of her estate, but of the brick wall which seemed to confront him whenever he tried to probe into the past.

Only three years ago, old Lessinger, who had known Martha all her life, had died; his nephew was comparatively new to the law and the practice. He was thirty-one, well-dressed, brisk, clean-cut—and he stood on the other side of an immeasurable gulf from Simon Coll. A public school, Cambridge, years in London studying law, contrasted sharply with life in a Dorset village.

Dorothy was expecting Simon at six o'clock; they would drive in to see the solicitor, then go to a film, and drive back. He neared the shop, his footsteps slackening, the pleasure he had once felt turned to an uneasy sense of guilt.

He raised his head as the Weymouth bus, which ran every two hours, came to a halt. With a sudden, uncontrollable impulse, he burst into a sprint, and leapt on to the platform as it began to move off. Dorothy, standing by the side of the three-wheeler, stared at him as if at a ghost. She would think he had gone mad. And perhaps he had. All he knew was that he could not marry Dorothy. He now looked back on that evening after the funeral as if upon an imagined horror, that had not, and could not have, happened.

As he paid his fare and settled into a corner seat, the picture of Dorothy's astonished face was before his mind's eye. For a while the thought that she would draw up alongside, or pass the bus, obsessed him, but she did not.

Once in Weymouth, Simon crossed the road to Lessinger's office, which he could identify only because it was two doors removed from the biggest hotel on the sea front. His hand was on the bell of the tall, Regency house, when the door opened. Lessinger stood there, in flannels and a sports shirt.

He shook hands.

"Forgive my unbusinesslike attire, but I've a tennis date later in the evening." He led the way into a large room, with padded leather chairs, bookcases and shelves packed with black boxes. Sitting behind a big, flat-topped desk, he drew a file of papers bound up in red tape towards him. "Now, here are the documents in the case. I don't know how much you were expecting in the estate, and I hope you won't be disappointed."

"I haven't given it much thought," Simon said.

"A very unusual attitude, if I may say so," said Lessinger, smiling. "Well now, when everything's taken into consideration and all the bills have been paid for the—ah—obsequies, there is a total residue of four thousand and seven pounds. A little estate duty is payable—let's say three thousand nine hundred pounds, and you're quite safe."

Simon said, astonished: "I'd no idea she had so much."

At first, the figure simply seemed a large, even a bewildering one, but as he sat there looking at the solicitor, he began to breathe more agitatedly, began to understand that he possessed what many people would call a small fortune. And it made no sense. Where had Aunt Martha got that amount of money? She had often laughed about scraping by on her school teacher's salary, and in later years he had believed that the few pounds a week he contributed towards the household expenses had been all-important to her.

She could never have saved up as much as four thousand pounds out of her salary.

Simon said huskily: "I can hardly believe it. How could she get hold of so much?"

"There I can't help at all," said Lessinger. "I can only tell you how much there was in securities at the bank for her. Much of the money is in National Savings Certificates, and they've appreciated in value quite a lot, of course."

"It's so much more than I dreamt she had."

Lessinger smiled kindly.

"I must say it's a pleasure to deal with someone who doesn't expect ten times as much as he gets. If you don't mind my saying so, Mr. Coll, there's a lot in common between you and your aunt —judging from my recollection of what my uncle told me about her."

Simon said: "Is there?" He settled back in his chair. "Mr. Lessinger, have you been through all the documents? Every one?" he demanded.

"Thoroughly, I assure you. And you're quite free to study them and ask me questions on anything that seems vague or incomprehensible."

"Then may I ask you if you found anything there to identify me?" Simon asked.

Lessinger's hand, still fiddling with the papers, stopped instantly. He sat very still, as if in complete surprise at the question.

Then he said: "There is no birth certificate, if that's what you mean. There is a letter from your aunt to my uncle, saying that she is ready to take out formal adoption papers, and adding that you are the son of her only sister, and that your name is Simon Coll. She charged my uncle not to give this information to the police, presumably to protect her dead sister's good name. That's the lot, I'm afraid."

"Everything?"

"Yes," Lessinger answered. "Did you expect anything else?"

"No," Simon said, slowly. "No, but I suppose I hoped there might be."

After a minute's silence, Lessinger said:

"Aren't you satisfied with the explanation given?"

Simon hesitated.

"No," he said at last, "no, I'm not satisfied. Because it doesn't make sense. Do you think it does? There's no birth certificate, and only adoption papers—I always understood that before an adoption a birth certificate was needed. Isn't that right?"

"If a child is a foundling, a certificate is issued to say so, and that's what happened. Mind telling us why you've suddenly come round to wondering?"

Simon turned his back to the window.

"I suppose it was the death of Aunt Martha. Or else——" He hesitated again, and looked into the other's face. He had never seen him as a human being before, only as a rather earnest, formally dressed solicitor. Now, quite unexpectedly, Simon found himself talking of his earlier doubts and his almost superficial wonderings, then of Aunt Martha's accident, and finally of Dorothy's comment about the coincidence of Coll and the Coll. By the time he had finished Simon was walking about the room, all feeling of strangeness and diffidence gone.

". . . so of course, I want to know who I am, who my parents were. I suppose the truth is that it didn't seem to matter during Aunt Martha's life. I didn't realise how much I took her for granted, how much she did for me. She was my whole background."

He broke off.

Lessinger said: "Yes, I know. I can imagine, anyhow. And the old brigade of Dern Abbas can't or won't talk?"

Simon said: "I'm sure that Mr. Fraill was astonished by my doubts when I talked to him about it—I'm sure he believed Aunt Martha's story, and if he did, then everyone in the village would,

13

too." He was clenching and unclenching his hands. "It will give you an idea how naïve I am when I tell you that until I got here this evening, it didn't occur to me that I might be able to find out more from my aunt's solicitor."

"Naïve?" Lessinger echoed. "Well, that's one word. Coll, I wish I could tell you what you want to know, but I can't. I'm not even sure that I ought to tell you what little I do know."

Simon stood still; heart thumping.

"You do know something, then?"

"A hint or two, that's all," Lessinger said, his expression changing to one of anxiety. "It's simply that when your aunt died I had to destroy an envelope which had been in her deed box. There was an instruction on it, written and signed by your aunt, instructing my uncle—and that means the firm, of course—to destroy it unopened on her death unless the instruction was cancelled. It never was."

Simon stood, tense and silent.

"The envelope was octavo size—nothing very important to look at," Lessinger said. "It was fairly thick, and the contents were quite small. To the casual touch, I'd say that they included a piece of ribbon, or tape." When Simon didn't speak or move, he went on a little uneasily: "I hope I've done the right thing in telling you. I felt you'd rather know than be fooled or lied to."

"Yes," Simon said, slowly. "I'm very grateful." He stepped closer to the desk. "Will you do something for me? You know the ropes, and you know how to start a search for—something like this. My parents, I mean. Will you dig as deep as you can?"

Lessinger didn't respond at once. Simon studied him, trying to assess the reason for his hesitation, aware of a fierce excitement; he felt almost as if he were on the verge of a great discovery, but also that the answer to his questions might give him cause for fear.

"Well, will you or won't you?" he demanded.

Lessinger said: "Simon, if I say 'yes' it will become an official search, and expensive. There's no need to throw your money about. Why don't you have a go yourself? I can tell you where to start—over at the offices of the *Globe*. The date on this envelope was 1937—January 14th, 1937—so that would be the date to look for. Then you could see if there was any report of a foundling. For instance, of a baby left——" He broke off.

"At one of the caves at the Coll," Simon said, thinly.

"Well, it's an obvious possibility," Lessinger told him. "And I can see that this thing goes deep in you. You won't be satisfied until you find out what you can, will you?"

"I certainly won't."

"Then search the *Globe* files—or better still, go and see old Joe Taggart, who was then the editor of the *Globe*. He edited it for forty years, and he was an old friend of my uncle. He's steeped deeper in local lore than any man I know. If you like, I'll telephone and make sure he'll be in this evening."

Simon said: "I'll be very glad if you will."

He watched Lessinger stretch out for the telephone, and his eyes were shining. He saw the other man dial, heard the ringing sound, and the sudden break in it.

"Mr. Taggart?" Lessinger asked, and murmured for a minute or so into the receiver before looking up at Simon. "Can you give him any idea of what time?"

"Straight away," Simon said.

Lessinger nodded. Presently he rang off.

"He's just going to start supper, so half-past eight will suit him better than eight o'clock." Lessinger scribbled on a slip of paper. "That's his address—in Quay Street. He's got a flat which overlooks the harbour. It's only five minutes' walk away from here."

Simon stood squarely in front of the desk.

"Mr. Lessinger, why have you been so helpful?"

Lessinger shifted back in his chair, hesitated, and then said with a flippancy which obviously cloaked more serious feeling:

"I like the look of you, and—well, confound it, in your position I should probably do the same. You look the type who'll be able to take it if, when you get to the bottom of the hole you're proposing to dig, what you find isn't exactly what you hoped to find."

Simon found himself smiling.

"I'll take it," he said. "I'll have to. Thank you very much." He held out his hand.

"Glad I could do something," Lessinger said. "Look here, why not come and have a meal with me tomorrow—no, not tomorrow. Friday, say. Then we can talk over anything you've learned from Old Joe. Seven o'clock—in the bar next door? I'll fix a table."

"Thank you," said Simon. "I'd like that."

Leaving the office, his eye fell on Dorothy's three-wheeler, double-parked outside the house.

Chapter 3

OLD MAN'S MEMORY

Dorothy was sitting at the wheel, and the reproach in her eyes was deep and hurtful. Simon knew that the conflict he had foreseen for a long time was upon him. He felt calmer about it than he had expected; deeply sorry; and yet quite sure of what he had to tell her. She didn't speak as he rounded the little vehicle, opened the door and slid in beside her.

"Will you park somewhere, Dot? I'd like to talk to you." When she didn't respond, he went on: "I feel that I owe you an explanation." The hackneyed conventionality of the words distressed him.

"You certainly owe me that," she said.

He had never known such sharpness in her voice, and when he looked at her, he saw her full lips tighten into a thin straight line. She was obviously fighting to restrain not hurt but anger. In the back of his mind, awaiting attention, lay the new things he had learned about Martha; but the problem of Dorothy had to be dealt with first. She drove slowly along the promenade, turned off towards the station, and found easy parking away from the crowds. All her movements were very deliberate as she stopped the car, and switched off the ignition.

"Well?" she said.

Her manner, her tone of voice, denoted a side of her he had not seen before. He turned round in his seat to face her, being careful not to touch her bare arm.

"Dorothy," he said. "I'm terribly sorry, but I've got to work things out for myself, and by myself. I've got to find out who I am before I can make up my mind where I'm going or what I'm going to do. I'm sorry that I walked out on you this evening, but I simply had to be alone."

"Well," she said, "that's a fine thing."

"Dorothy——"

"I suppose you won't object if I have *my* say," she interrupted. He saw that thinness at her lips again, the way they turned down at the corners, and realised there was a capacity for spitefulness in her which he had never suspected. "If there's one thing I can't stand, it's downright rudeness."

"Dot, I tell you that I had to be on my own."

She said: "But there are some things you don't want on your own, aren't there? You were glad enough to have me around a few nights ago, or don't you remember that little incident?"

"I remember," Simon said. "I shall always remember, but—"

Her eyes blazed into fury, her voice became shrill.

"What do you mean, *but*? You had your way with me, you can't just shrug that off. You and I have got to get married, and damned soon, because if anything should happen as a result of the other night, we don't want all the village talking. It's past time you left the Fraills, anyhow—slaving away for that old miser for a pittance when you can earn twice as much if you come into the business. There's a shop over at Iwerne which is going for a song; we can have two shops within a month, if we're sensible. Before we turn round we'll have three or four, and before we know where we are we can have a chain of stores. That's what I've always dreamed about, and if you've any guts that's what you'll dream about, too . . ."

She broke off suddenly; perhaps it was the expression in his eyes which changed her nagging resentment to alarm.

"Si!" she exclaimed. "Don't look at me like that. Si, what are you thinking about? Si!"

"I've told you, Dot," he said, and now he rested his hand on her arm. "I'm sorry, terribly sorry, especially after the other evening, but I've got to find out who I am. That will probably mean leaving the village, it may mean—well, who can tell? Before I can even think of settling down again I've got to find out all I can about myself."

"But—but Simon, you can't leave the village! We're going to get married; everyone knows it. Simon, you're upset, you don't know what you're saying."

"I know, Dot," Simon said.

"But you can't leave me now, you simply can't!"

"Listen, Dorothy, I don't know how long it will take or where it will take me, but until I've found out, I can't tell what I'm going to do."

"But you promised to marry me!"

"I didn't, Dorothy," Simon said gently.

"You mean to say that you did what you have done, without meaning to marry me?" There was rage and fright in her eyes, but strong forces held her back—perhaps real fear that if she were not careful he would really be lost to her.

"Dorothy, I wish I felt differently," he said. "I wish I knew my

17

own mind as certainly as you do yours, but I don't. I've got to get away from Dern Abbas. I've spent my life there, but it's come to be a prison. I've got to go away, and search——"

"You don't know what you're talking about," she said, and caught her breath. "And don't think I don't know what you really mean, either." Now, anger was rising to the surface, and he felt almost glad of it. "You've always thought yourself superior to anyone in the village, you and your so-called *Aunt* Martha, her and her airs. She couldn't have been any better than she should have been, and she didn't even dare to own up to you. Who do you think you're fooling?"

Simon said softly: "Is that the village talk?"

"Why, my mum and dad heard that before we'd been in the village a month!"

"Did they?" asked Simon. He felt unnaturally calm as he looked at the girl, and glad of the calm; to lose his temper now would be the final folly and the final injustice, too. "Well, I'm going to find out whether it's true or not, Dorothy, no matter how long it takes me."

"And when you know, what difference is that going to make? What good do you think it will do you?"

"I wish I knew," Simon said.

Dorothy drew in a deep breath, and clenched her hands. It would not have surprised him had she struck him; and he would not have blamed her. Then slowly her eyes began to lose their fire, and fear crept back again.

"Simon," she said. "I didn't mean to talk like that. I—I love you so much, I can't bear the thought of losing you. Promise me you'll come back as soon as you can. Promise me."

At least she knew, now, that he was going from the village.

"I'll be back," he said. "I'll be back, one day."

It was on the tip of his tongue to say that when he came back she'd probably have a husband and children, but he checked himself. Then he realised that without having thought about it, he expected to be away for a long, long time. Since he had left Lessinger's office, he had known that. Aunt Martha had given him enough money to go and search, and he felt that her sanction and approval had been given with it.

"Oh, Si!" Dorothy began; and tears welled up in her eyes.

*　　*　　*

She left him almost abruptly, and his chief reaction was one of great relief. He watched the little red car turn the corner towards Dorchester, and waited for a stream of traffic before crossing the road. As he walked slowly towards the harbour, the smell of frying onions following him, teasing him, from a nearby stall, it reminded him that he was hungry. He was eating his second hotdog when he realised that after the car had gone from his sight, he had not given Dorothy a thought. That was how callous he could be, how little she really mattered. The hour on the Coll seemed like something which had taken place an age ago, not just a few days.

He did not much like himself for this indifference, but he had acquired a basic honesty from Aunt Martha—the ability to look at himself with a dispassionate eye. He could take no pride or satisfaction in what had happened, but he could not lie himself into false emotions, either. He would see her again, for he had some clearing-up to do at the farm, but all relationship, both physical and emotional, was over between them. Finished. Dead. He walked briskly towards the quay. Number 75 was near the end, one of a line of tall, terraced houses, marked almost uniformly by cards bearing the words: *Bed and Breakfast*, *Apartments*, or *No Vacancy*. Simon pressed the top bell of three, which had the name Taggart written beside it in red ink, and almost at once a nondescript woman appeared, directing him to a closed door up two flights of stairs.

Taggart himself answered his knock, leading him with a slow, arthritic step to a room overlooking the harbour. Two easy chairs were drawn up on either side of the window.

"Sit down, Mr. Coll," Taggart said. "My wife'll bring some coffee in soon—or would you rather have a beer?"

"A beer, if I may."

"Thought so, from the look of you," said Taggart. He sat back heavily in his chair, grunting as if with twinges of pain. He had a long, thin, deeply-lined face, dark-tanned, unshaven. "So you're young Coll," he observed. "I knew your aunt, as you know. Remarkable woman, Martha Tenby, no right to waste herself in a godforsaken spot like Dern Abbas. Woman with her education and talents should have been in a university city, where she could find minds to match her own. Told her so."

"I think she was a happy woman, sir," Simon said.

"Happy? Yes, probably. Don't know, though—depends what you mean by happiness. So many definitions. Ah, well, you didn't come to hear me pontificating, and that's just about all I can do now. Can't write for more than half-an-hour at a stretch. I always

19

wanted to write a history of this part of Dorset, fascinating part of England—know much about it?"

"A little, sir," Simon said.

"That's about all anyone knows," Taggart asserted. He broke off as the door opened, and a woman came in, younger than Taggart by at least twenty years.

Simon stood up.

"Please sit down," said Mrs. Taggart. She spoke with an air of brittle gaiety that could have been assumed. She put the tray she was carrying down on a table between them and went on: "Joe, I'm going next door to see Lucy Partwell, I won't be more than an hour. I may see you when I get back, Mr. Coll."

The old man sighed as she closed the door.

"Pour me out some coffee, will you?" he asked gruffly. "Help yourself to beer." He waited; and when he took the cup his fingers trembled, but he managed to lift it to his lips. "I've been thinking," he said. "Thinking. Since Lessinger telephoned me. How much do you want to know, Simon Coll?"

"I simply want to know who I am."

"Fair question," conceded Taggart. "Can't answer it, though." Simon's heart beat loud in painful expectancy. "It was January, 1936—don't tell me what a good memory I've got, I telephoned the night clerk at the *Globe* office and he dug out the date for me. January 17th, 1936." He hesitated, and half-closed his eyes, as if memory were clouding, and Simon sat with the beer in his hand, his body rigid. The periwinkle blue eyes opened abruptly, and Taggart said: "Sure you want to know what I can tell you?"

"Yes, sir."

"Right," said Taggart. "Man has every right to know the truth about himself. If he is wise to dig for it, is another matter—but don't let me wander away from the subject! On the late afternoon of January 17th, 1936, the story goes, Martha Tenby was walking along the top of the Coll when she heard a child crying. Going to investigate, she found the baby, dressed warmly in knitted clothes, lying in one of the caves. There was the usual envelope pinned to the jacket—would some kind person look after it? So some kind person did—our Martha Tenby."

Taggart seemed to sense Simon's tension, for his voice became gentler.

"It was a Saturday. The *Globe* doesn't publish on Sunday, of course, and by Monday, we'd had a flood of local and national news. The baby had a little paragraph to itself, that was all. I kept Martha's name out of it as she asked me to. No one made any difficulties—no reason why they should. Adoption papers were made out in the name of Coll, which seemed suitable then, and Martha Tenby acquired a son. There were the usual rumours, of course, inseparable from villages. Still, most of the people who knew Martha knew better than to believe that the baby was hers."

The old man stopped.

"Can you be sure of that?" demanded Simon.

"Sure of it? Of course I'm sure," said Taggart testily. "Certain inescapable physical evidence when a woman's pregnant you know! Martha had been in Dern Abbas for seven months without a break, under the very discerning eyes of the villagers. Nothing, believe me, in that line would have escaped them. Some things are beyond all doubt, and the fact that you weren't Martha's son is one of them. However—there were certain peculiar features."

"And they were?"

"Well, the baby was well cared-for, about a month old, and had been recently fed. When Martha found it, it was half-past three, and at that time of year getting on for dark. Not a time, or a place, one would suppose, to choose for an evening stroll in winter. Can be devilish wild up there. So there remains the possible inference that your Aunt Martha went there by arrangement. Can't be sure, but—that's what it looked like to me."

"Then if you're right, she knew my mother," Simon said.

"Yes," Taggart agreed. "Or else she knew that you were going to be stranded. Never a woman to do much by chance or on the spur of the moment, your Aunt Martha. And there were one or two other factors. I remember them well. She was rather edgy about that time—very averse to the publicity, and anxious to get the adoption through as quickly as possible. I don't think she was the kind of woman to adopt a foundling without a great deal of thought. In fact I'm sure of it. But there was one other curious feature. I don't know whether anyone else knew of it—except my old friend Arthur Lessinger, who acted for Martha." The old man paused again, then spoke with certainty and deliberation.

"In that envelope was money. Dollars. I don't know how much —Lessinger banked it, right away. But I know there were at least ten notes. Could have been one dollar bills—or it could have been one hundred dollar bills, which would make a thousand dollars, a lot of money in those days. How do I know? Simple, young man, simple. The envelope was torn when it was taken off the baby's clothes. I saw the green printing—yes, I would say there were at least a thousand dollars."

Old Taggart stared at Simon, his eyes a piercing blue.

Chapter 4

SOLDIER ... SAILOR

Simon said: "I can't tell you how grateful I am, sir." He felt that the words came out awkwardly, but he could not help himself. The blue eyes held great intelligence—but did they hold any more secrets? "Is that—is that everything you can tell me?"

"No," said Taggart, slowly, "not quite. Rest is guess work, though, even more guess work than the money."

"I'd like to hear."

"Sure you would," Taggart said. "Well—go down to the *Globe* office. Get out the issues for 1935 and 1936. You'll find that there was an American man-of-war stationed at Portland during that period. Part of some exchange scheme, don't know what it was— the Admiralty was even more cagey than it is now. However, there were five hundred or so American sailors and a hundred and twenty American marines stationed at Portland and nearby from February 1935 to January 1936. Early February. Can you count?"

"Ten months," Simon said.

"That's right—ten months. Time for nature to take its course, eh? The ship completed its mission and sailed back for America on January 21st, 1936. Two days after you were found. Mind you, this doesn't necessarily mean anything, but it might mean a great deal."

"Yes," Simon said, huskily. "It certainly could."

"Name of the ship—*Chespeak*. Commander Ronald Martenson, in command—he was killed four years later. Atlantic Convoy. I never could remember the names of the other officers, but I do remember a tall young rating—named Laughing Water Smith. Can you believe that? Great tall fellow, face as dark as a bronze statue, high nose—said to be half Navajo Indian and half white, but you know how these stories get around and I believe a ship is even more of a gossip shop than a village like Dern Abbas. Laughing Water Smith was the Commander's steward, very knowledgeable and very discreet. What I'm saying to you, my boy, is that you would probably get more out of that rating than you would out of an officer and a gentleman. But whether Laughing Water lived through the war or not, I don't know. The *Chespeak* was sunk with most hands—and I always understood

22

that a lot of the chaps who were here with her also went down. The marines on board were stationed at Weymouth, a lot of the time. I'm told the marine casualties in the war were very high, very high indeed. Still, if you're really interested there's something to go on, and I always found the American authorities friendly and willing to be helpful. They might have changed by now, of course, but—well! That's all I can tell you, Simon Coll."

"Thank you, sir," Simon said.

"Except perhaps one thing."

"Yes?" Simon asked.

"Ever seen many Americans?" Taggart demanded.

"No, sir."

"Well, take a look at them when you can," advised Taggart. "They vary, of course, and there are plenty of stocky, tubby ones, but most of those marines came from the South-West. Lean-hipped, long-shanked types. You've that kind of body, Simon Coll. Six feet two, aren't you?"

"Six one," Simon corrected.

"Well, well, it may not mean anything, but it could mean a lot." Taggart touched Simon's arm. "Hope I haven't talked too much. The truth is, it's always stuck in my mind. A newspaper man always wants the answers, you know. Why should Martha do what she did—but I've talked enough, quite enough! Now you know what I know, what do you think about it?"

Simon said: "I haven't had time to think, yet."

"No. I suppose not. Going to take a look at the United States?"

"Very likely, sir."

"Lucky young pup," said Taggart, gruffly. "I always wanted to go there, but when I could have gone I couldn't afford it, and when I could afford it this blasted arthritis had got me. If you do go over there, if you find out anything, I want to know. Understand me? I want to know."

"I'll make sure you do," Simon said. As he stood up, he became aware of the outside world for the first time since Taggart had started to talk. The sea was greying over; there were few people at the water's edge, fewer walking the quays. A faint haze filled the horizon—the horizon which would recede further and further until it reached the east coast of America. "One more thing, Mr. Taggart."

"Yes?"

"Who else would know anything about this? Old Mr. Lessinger is dead, and——"

23

"Catchpole, Aunt Martha's bank manager, died eleven years ago. You're lucky I'm still alive!" The bright blue eyes twinkled.

"I—I'm extremely grateful." Simon hesitated, his mind suddenly filled with questions, but he saw that the old man was very tired. "Can I let myself out, Mr. Taggart?"

"Yes, you can find your way," the old man said. "I never walk far unless I have to." He grinned, and added: "Or unless I want to!"

Simon left him leaning back in his chair and looking out towards the haze-dimmed sea.

*　　*　　*

Simon walked along the promenade, jostled by crowds coming off the beach, and was hardly aware of them. He was conscious of the way he walked, but he had never given it a thought before. Was old Taggart right? Did he walk 'like an American'? Was an old man's memory playing tricks? Very little played Taggart tricks, that was certain; he could take everything that had been said at its face value. And none of it was really strange.

He could remember Aunt Martha's interest in and enthusiasm for the United States as clearly as if she were talking to him now. Had she in fact been there? He couldn't believe she had, or she would have told him. Had she relatives there? He had never heard of relatives, except the 'sister' whose child he was supposed to be.

He reached the clock, and stared across the road at Lessinger's office. The only bitter thing was the fact that Lessinger had actually destroyed that envelope which could have explained so much. But now that he had started searching, it was astonishing that he had learned as much as he had.

He could picture that cave, the wrapped baby, and the pinned envelope of dollar notes. He could picture the American sailors and marines who would spend a lot of their time in Weymouth—and there had been thousands of American soldiers billeted in Dorset during the war. Up to his eighth year he could remember them as big, tall, brown-clad figures. The imagined figure of a bronzed, hook-nosed man called Laughing Water Smith was much more vivid than any individual he had known in his childhood.

He heard someone calling: "Simon."

It was like a voice out of the past, out of a different world. He felt his jaws tightening, and he did not want to stop, but he

24

would have to. Exasperation, anger, and an uneasy sense of guilt were all mixed up in him.

"*Simon!*"

Dorothy was just behind him. He must have passed her, unnoticing. Perhaps that accounted for the shocked tone of her voice. He glanced round. She was very near. He wished she wouldn't look so anxious, so tense. Even her lips seemed white.

"Simon," she repeated, and drew level with him. "I—I thought you were going to ignore me."

"I didn't see you," he said.

"But you walked right past me!"

"I'm—I'm sorry." He walked on a few steps. "Dorothy, it's no use. I can't help myself." He did not intend to tell her what he had learned from Taggart; she was the last person in the world to talk to about that. "I just didn't see you. I'm sorry."

She gave him a sly, sidelong glance, and slid her arm under his. He could feel the softness of her breast, and knew that the pressure was deliberate; and he remembered how she had stood at the top of the Coll with the wind beating against her body, sculpting every line. He fought against a desire to snatch his arm free and stride ahead; he could outwalk her in a few seconds, she would have no chance of catching up.

"Simon, we mustn't quarrel," she went on. "I couldn't stand it if we parted bad friends. Let me drive you home, it will give us time to talk things over."

There was nothing to talk over. It would be wiser to walk on, now, and put an end to it for good, but—why hurt more than he must? He did not really understand her except in one thing; she was fighting to keep him with whatever weapons she knew.

"Please, Si," she begged.

"If that's what you want, of course I'll come," he said.

"Oh, I'm so glad, Si! The car's just across the road."

There was a lighter, brighter note in her voice. She took his hand as they waited at the kerb for a stream of traffic, and held it tightly as they crossed; she wasn't going to let him go. He had made a serious mistake.

He opened the door for her, and she got in; by accident or intent, her skirt caught against the door handle, and was pulled right back. Her big, round, creamy leg showed almost to the top of the thigh. She gave a little laugh as she unhooked the dress. Simon closed the door and went round the other side. He hesitated, then got into the car.

She was excited and delighted, as if this were a major victory.

Out on the hilly meadowland she slowed down. She turned off the road into a field behind a high hedge, stopping the car.

"Let's talk about the situation now, Simon. It's a lovely spot here, and we're all alone." She leaned towards him, pressing against him. "Why don't we lie down on the grass, and just talk about things? You know how much I love you, don't you? There isn't anything I wouldn't do for you."

She opened her door and climbed down, and he stepped out on his side. She came round to meet him, hands outstretched, the plunging line of her bosom overprominent. He realised what a voluptuary she was, what kind of physical ecstasy she would always be able to give—and he realised too how sure she was of the magnetism of her body.

"Dorothy," he said, "if I could love anybody, it would be you, but before I can think of anything else, I've got to find out who and what I am. Don't you understand? I want you, I want to stay with you, but it wouldn't be fair to either of us. I've got to go."

"Si!" she exclaimed. "Si, no, don't go, don't go——"

He strode away from her, ignoring the hands that clutched, the stormy breathing. He went through the gateway and along the road, then across the hills towards Dern Abbas. Over to the south-west, the Coll looked mountainous against the dying sky. He did not hear Dorothy again, did not even hear the engine of the car start up. After this, she would hate him, of course; she would hate him because he had spurned her body. He remembered the night when he had not, and wondered if that folly would turn into a shadow as big and dark and menacing as the shadow of the Coll.

* * *

"Mr. Fraill," he said, an hour later, "I hope you'll forgive me, but I've got to leave the village right away. I—I'm not going to marry Dorothy, and it will be very embarrassing for her if I——" He didn't finish.

The old man said: "You must do whatever you think best, Simon. You will always have my good wishes. When did you plan to go?"

"I ought to leave in the morning," Simon answered. "It won't take me long to pack, and Mr. Lessinger will look after the cottage and Aunt Martha's things."

"Won't you come back at all, my boy?" The old man sounded shocked.

"One day," Simon said. "Yes, of course, one day." He hesitated, and then went on: "Thank you, Mr. Fraill, for all you've done for me."

Chapter 5

SHOCK QUESTION

Everyone at the offices of the *Globe* was much younger, brisker, more business-like than Taggart, and none of those to whom Simon spoke on the Friday morning seemed really interested, but after he had looked through the files of old newspapers, some of them yellowed with age, he was aware of an elderly, rather portly man watching him.

Simon made a few pencilled notes, and turned to go. The plump man came forward with a smile. Then Simon recognised him as a reporter who had interviewed him after Aunt Martha's accident.

"My name's Rinson, the oldest hack on the *Globe*," the plump man informed him. "Old Joe Taggart taught me my job, and editors don't come any better. He had a word with me on the telephone last night."

Simon's interest sharpened.

"Asked me to give you what help I could, but I was out when you arrived," said Rinson. "There's one thing that I think you ought to know, Mr. Coll, although the police would probably want my blood if they knew I'd talked to you about it."

Simon said: "Police? Where do the police come in?" His thoughts went swiftly back to the days following the accident, the enquiries, the fact that the driver who had knocked Aunt Martha down had not stopped, and had never been traced.

"In a way they don't," said Rinson, with a peculiar little smile. "As a matter of fact, Mr. Coll, I've inquired into a lot of hit and run accidents, it's part of my job. The police did discover that a stolen car was used, you'll remember, but the driver was never traced. The car was found in a car park at Southampton." Simon could almost see the paragraph in the *Globe*, reporting this. "There was a possibility that the driver went away on a ship," Rinson was saying. "I took the trouble to find out which ships.

left the docks that night. Apart from a couple of coasting vessels, only one did, Mr. Coll."

Simon asked, thinly: "Which one?"

"An American passenger liner, called the *New States*," answered Rinson, and when Simon made no comment, he went on with a deprecating shrug: "I told the police all this, but there was absolutely no evidence. However, they checked with the coasters, and cleared both crews, and then checked with the American shipping company. On that particular night, a dozen of the *New States* crew arrived very late. Most of these were paid off in New York, at the end of the trip," declared Rinson. "If there'd been any real evidence that a Yankee sailor had been in that car the police would have taken it further, but they couldn't work on a guess—not even an intelligent guess."

Simon said: "Why are you telling me this?"

"Because you're interested in your past, and the only person who could have told you anything about it died after that so-called accident," Rinson declared quietly. "What's more, there was an American angle to your—what's the word?—adoption. I told Joe Taggart about it, when he called me, and he said you ought to know. I'm not interested in any story angle, but if you feel like talking about it, any time—well, here's my card."

"I appreciate it very much," Simon said. "I'll probably get in touch."

*　　*　　*

He tried to concentrate on other inquiries, and made several, but Rinson's story kept surging to the front of his mind. He felt that he had to talk to someone about it, and was impatient for the evening, when he was to dine with Lessinger.

*　　*　　*

"Well, Simon," Lessinger said, "what have you been doing with yourself today?"

His manner was brisk and rather breezy, his use of Simon's Christian name unexpected, but apparently natural. Now he moved towards the American bar.

"How about a drink before we go and eat?"

"I'm not much on short drinks," Simon said. "But don't let me stop you."

"Right, well we'll have something at the table. I'm not much

28

of a cocktail man either, unless it's at a party. I've got a table booked." Lessinger led the way to the dining-room, and a waiter who obviously knew him well took them to a window seat. Lessinger gave a rapid and concise order, then settled back in his chair. "I gather that Joe Taggart really whetted your appetite."

"He did indeed. I've spent most of the day at the *Globe* office."

Lessinger looked startled.

"Day off from the farm?"

"I've left the farm."

Lessinger said, almost wistfully: "Well, you certainly move fast. Had any luck?"

"No," Simon said slowly. It was surprisingly difficult to broach Rinson's story. "I've managed to get copies of everything that appeared in the newspaper Mr. Taggart told me about, and I've read all the reports there were about the American sailors and marines at Portland around that time. There weren't many names." He settled back in his chair, feeling much less ill-at-ease in the comparatively luxurious surroundings than he had expected. "There were several names of men who got drunk or had accidents, and an unknown sailor was known to have killed a townsman in a drunken brawl. The Captain of the Marines was a man named Evans. The Commander of the ship was a Captain Dellafont." Simon was talking almost to himself. "Then I discovered that the Mayor of Weymouth that year knew my aunt, and he's still alive."

"They live long in the sunny south-west," said Lessinger. "Who is it?"

"Alderman Pike."

"Not a bad old boy," Lessinger said. "Could he help you?"

"No, not really," Simon said. "He didn't remember anyone but the two men I've mentioned; it's all a bit vague to him. He told me of several other people who knew the Americans—the Town Clerk, for instance. He lives out at Upway."

"Any luck?"

"Mr. Lessinger——"

"Guy," said Lessinger, easily, turning his attention to a selection of hors d'oeuvre. "You know, you're a mystery in more ways than one. You've been buried in Dern Abbas all your life, the original country bumpkin, but when it's necessary to break out, you're a natural. Don't mind me. Like this paté?"

Simon said absently: "It looks good." His mind was on Rinson's theory, and he went on doggedly: "The truth is, it's difficult to tell anybody exactly what I want."

"I can imagine," Lessinger said drily. "You can't very well show them a copy of the bit in the *Globe*, and say: 'That's me, do you know who was responsible?' "

Simon laughed.

"That's about how I feel."

"The real trouble is knowing where to start, I suppose."

"Yes," Simon said. "I'd like to find out if any of the officers or men on the *Chespeak* married local girls, or——"

Lessinger smiled drily.

"Didn't marry them!"

Simon laughed outright.

"You take it pretty light-heartedly."

"Simon," said Lessinger, "that's really why I suggested dinner tonight. I've got the idea that you're a bit weighed down by all this. You needn't be, you know. I'd hate to think that you were carrying a chip on your shoulder. You're not really the type, yet you do seem to be taking the situation pretty dourly. I thought if we could have a *tête-a-tête* tonight I could find out how much I dare say to you, and as you've gathered, it's plenty." He grinned broadly. "What I'm really saying, I suppose, is that if you want to start investigating, that's fine, but get all the fun you can out of doing it."

Simon didn't speak.

"If I've said too much——" Lessinger began quietly.

"No, not a word too much," Simon said. "I can imagine Aunt Martha saying almost the same thing. What I can't understand is that she should hide everything from me—but, well, I might discover the answer to that, too. Can you find out for me whether she has any living relatives?"

"I'll try," Lessinger said.

They both turned appreciatively to their *sole meunière*, then Lessinger murmured ruminatively:

"Exactly what do you hope to find out locally?"

"Whether any of these sailors or marines married over here, or had an *affaire*."

"Yes," said Lessinger. "The obvious. But face all the facts, won't you? If your father was one of these men, he made a good job of hushing it up, and a good job of getting Aunt Martha to help. If Aunt Martha knew your mother, it's more than likely that she would have kept up some kind of correspondence or association. Yet the fact remains that she didn't—did she?"

"There's no indication at all that she did."

"Right, then. The fact that she didn't, suggests that the girl

30

concerned—your mother—kept it from her family. So, the family wouldn't be likely to know. The birth wasn't in a hospital or nursing home; if it had been it would have been registered. So there isn't much hope of breaking the veil of silence around here, is there? If your aunt went to such lengths to help hush it up——"

"You've made your point," Simon interrupted.

"Agree?"

"Of course."

"Well?"

Simon sipped the red wine, and found it a little bitter, but not unpleasant. He looked straight into Lessinger's eyes. He had to get Rinson's story off his chest. He couldn't hold it back any longer.

"There's something else, too," he said. "Do you know a man named Rinson, a reporter on the *Globe*?"

"I know him very well."

"Is he a sound man?"

"Very much so," Lessinger declared confidently. "Have you seen him in your travels?"

"Yes. He virtually said that he wondered if the man who knocked Aunt Martha down did it deliberately," Simon blurted out. "In other words, attempted murder."

Lessinger exclaimed: "Good God!"

"Had you thought of that?" demanded Simon.

Lessinger looked completely astounded.

"No, it hadn't crossed my mind, but this American angle——" he pushed his chair back. "I can't believe it."

Yet the expression in his eyes showed that he felt not only the shock, but also the possible significance of the story. It was some time before he recovered enough to say:

"Well, it's a possibility you have to keep in mind, I suppose. What are you planning to do?"

"Apart from booking a trip on board the *New States*, I'm going to check back to the days when I was left at the Coll," Simon answered. "I've already checked some of the references to the *Chespeak*, during the war—many of the crew when it was stationed at Portland did go down with it, and there's bound to be a casualty list. Once I can find out who died, I shall have some idea what kind of a task it will be to find those who are still alive. And it could be someone who made a trip on the *New States* a few months ago. I'll concentrate on the American side for the time being."

31

Lessinger said: "A hell of a problem."

"Well," Simon said, "I've got plenty of time, and four thousand pounds. If I'm careful, that should last me a few years. And I can always come back to farming!" For the first time this evening he thought of Dorothy, but it was only fleetingly. "I did wonder if it would help if I went to see the American Consul at Southampton. Think it would?"

"The Consul's in America, on leave," Lessinger said. "His stand-in is a nice young chap, but he'd have to refer everything to his Embassy, and they'd have to refer to Washington and the Navy Department."

"In other words, I'm wasting my time over here," Simon said.

"What you should do here is size the situation up and make a final decision on whether you want to go on with the search," Lessinger said, more seriously than he had spoken before. "After that, if your decision is what I fear it will be, I'd say that your best bet will be to go to Washington. And if you don't mind another word of advice from me before that fillet arrives——" he glanced towards the service door—"I'd travel first class and give yourself a complete change and rest. Ah!" A large silver dish was being borne to their table. Lessinger seemed glad to be able to change the subject. "They spoil me here. Don't those chipped potatoes look good!" He grinned. "In America, I understand, they're called French fries. Or had Aunt Martha told you that?"

"She'd told me," Simon said, slowly. "Will you ask the police if they did consider the possibility of a deliberate run down?"

"I thought you'd be after that," Lessinger said gruffly. "All right. In the morning."

*　　*　　*

At half-past eleven next day, Simon went to the solicitor's office.

"All I can tell you," Lessinger said, "is that Rinson told you the truth, but every hit and run case is investigated very thoroughly. Rinson's theory is a thousand to one chance."

"That's good enough," said Simon.

In the next ten days, he realised more and more how much Aunt Martha had taught him about America, and how much she herself had known. It was almost as if she had been making sure that when he did go there, he would not go as a complete stranger. The outside possibility of the 'accident' being intentional seemed to become more slender; but it continued to preoccupy him.

On the eleventh day, he sailed from Southampton on the *S.S. New States*, cabin class, in spite of Lessinger's advice.

By the evening, he began to realise how little he really knew about Americans, how different the living man was from the word pictures drawn about him. There was at least one disappointment, too. Nine men out of ten were short or squat; only here and there was there a tall, lean-shanked man, among the passengers or among the crew. But the few whom Simon did see had a curious way of walking, almost a cat-like way. It was as if they walked with complete assurance, and yet also with great caution; as if they were not quite sure what they would meet round the corner. And those who fitted this pattern which Joe Taggart had talked about all seemed very much the same: men of the early twenties to the middle thirties, clear-eyed, direct-looking, slow speaking, with accents which were quite unfamiliar. Undoubtedly there was a pattern, and with every day of the trip he became more aware of it.

He asked guarded questions of his room steward, only to learn that members of the crew who overstayed their shore leave were usually paid off in New York; there was nothing unusual about that. His questions about the *Chespeak* got him nowhere, and apart from one or two stewards, none of the crew he saw seemed old enough to have been in Southampton twenty-five years ago.

By the third day, he was as friendly with the seven people at his dining-table as with many people he had known all his life; and certainly knew them better than he did the two men with whom he shared an inside cabin. The casual friendliness of shipboard life was different from anything he had known, but it had an appeal which attracted him. It was easy to mention the *Chespeak* and the sailors and soldiers who had been stationed at Portland, as if casually.

At dinner on that third day, Clara Foreman, a fluffy-haired, jolly little woman from Alabama and her tall, massive husband, who spoke with an unbelievably slow drawl, slid into their seats opposite him.

"Simon, you just wouldn't believe it," she cried. "Josh, Simon just wouldn't believe the coincidence, would he?"

"I guess not," the man said.

"It must surely be one of the strangest coincidences you could imagine," his wife declared. "You never would believe it, Simon, but on C deck there's a cabin steward named Terry who served on

33

board that very ship, the one you were talking about last night."

Simon tried to cover a sudden, intense excitement.

"That—that's quite remarkable," he said. "Terry——" the words came out with difficulty—"Terry must be getting on by now."

"He certainly is. Well over sixty I should say," Clara speculated. "I told him that you came from the very place where the Chespeak was stationed, way back in the thirties, and he was real interested. Isn't that right, Josh? Why don't you come to our cabin and have a visit with him?"

"Will the steward be on duty?" Simon asked.

"He surely will, he'll be on duty until ten o'clock when the night stewards take over," Clara said. "And I asked him to stop by our cabin at nine o'clock. I'm sure he'll be very glad to meet you."

They strolled out of the dining-room, up to the promenade deck. The lounge was already crowded for bingo, the cage was turning, the numbers were being called out. Simon waited for the Foremans, patiently; there was no hurry about anything on board ship. Clara was stopped by a woman of her own age, with a gusty voice; Josh was drawn into the conversation.

"Simon, why don't you go down to our cabin? We won't be long," Clara called. "It's C 107." She waved her hand as if taking obedience for granted.

Simon walked down the stairs along the passage towards the Foremans' cabin, and saw a little group of white-clad stewards some distance away; two white men, two black. He wondered if by chance Terry, the steward who had been on the Chespeak, would be coloured. He knew the problem of the white and coloured races by the book, but only a few dozen times in his life had he seen men with black skins.

He reached the cabin, and turned the handle. One of the stewards broke away from the others and came towards him. The man was of medium height; he moved with a deceptive slowness. His hair was iron grey, close-cropped, and grew well back from a pale forehead. It was hard to believe that such a man had spent his life at sea.

He was frowning, as if shortsightedly. As he drew nearer, it seemed to Simon that his frown deepened. A groove appeared between his eyes, and he slackened his pace. He was perhaps ten feet away when he stopped still, staring at Simon—staring as a man might stare at the unbelievable. His lips parted. Simon heard

34

the sharp intake of his breath, and saw the way his hands clenched and tightened at his sides.

Neither of them spoke.

Chapter 6

STEWARD

At last, Simon broke the silence, and asked huskily: "Are you Steward Terry?" He was acutely aware of some significance in the way the other man looked at him. Words came out with difficulty. It seemed that he had been standing here for a long time, staring at this man.

The steward said: "Yes, sir, I'm Terry."

"Mr. and Mrs. Foreman have been delayed. They asked me to come and wait for them. I'm Simon Coll."

"Yes, sir, Mr. Coll." The man's voice was uneven, shaken. "Can I get you a drink, sir?"

"I'll wait for Mr. and Mrs. Foreman," Simon said.

"Sure, you do that," said Terry. "You do just that, Mr. Coll."

He turned back, and it seemed to Simon that his walk was quicker now; he moved with more urgency. Only the droning of the ship's engines sounded, and the steward's footsteps hastening away. The other three stewards were still standing together; it seemed to Simon that they were startled by Terry—certainly they were staring at him.

He heard one man say: "You okay, Terry?"

"Sure," Terry said. His voice was very faint. "Sure, I'm okay."

"You ain't seen a ghost, have you?" That was one of the coloured stewards, and he gave an easy, happy laugh.

Terry didn't answer.

Simon turned into the cabin. He crossed to the closed porthole, and dropped on to the corner of a bed. He stared at the open door, and seemed to see the steward's face, and to hear the coloured man's soft, carrying voice:

"You ain't seen a ghost, have you?"

That 'ghost' fitted into the obvious so clearly that there couldn't be any mistake; Terry had seen something in his face, some likeness out of the past——

"It can't be that!" Simon said, under his breath, and jumped up. He reached the passage, to call the steward, but none of them was in sight.

The Foremans and another couple were coming towards him. Simon waved to them, and turned towards the steward's quarters. He reached the serving galley. Three stewards were there; but not Terry.

"You want something, sir?" asked the coloured steward who had spoken to Terry.

"Is Terry here?" Simon asked.

"He just gone done burnt his hand, sir," the coloured steward said, in that soft, bewilderingly persuasive voice. "He had to go right up to the nurse to have that burn attended to. I don't imagine he will be on duty again tonight, sir, but if you require anything, I'll be happy to get it for you."

"Has he been a steward on this ship for long?"

"Yes, sir, for ten years I guess," the man answered.

The other two stewards, one black, one white, were staring at Simon. He hesitated and turned away.

". . . why, that's too bad, I declare it's too bad," Clara Foreman said, when Simon told her that Terry had gone off duty. "I do hope he hasn't burnt his hand badly, a burn can be very serious. Can't it, Josh?"

*   *   *

Simon lay on his back, wide awake. One of the other men was snoring faintly, the third was reading in his bunk, with the bunk light on. The ceiling was only a foot or two away from Simon's head. On it, he seemed to see Terry's face, the frown, the sudden astonishment.

"*You ain't seen a ghost, have you, Terry?*"

Ghost of whom?

And why should the steward be so shaken that he should turn and hurry away? Why had he pretended to, or purposely, injured his hand so that he could go off duty? For that had been an excuse, of course; for some reason a man who had served on board the *Chespeak* had been frightened by a 'ghost'. It hardly seemed to make sense, and yet nothing had been imagined; the man *had* virtually run away. Had he a guilty conscience? Could he have stolen that hit and run car?

It was two o'clock before Simon dropped off to sleep.

*   *   *

"No, sir, Mr. Coll," the coloured steward said. "Terry is not on duty, right now."

"No, sir," the other white steward said. "Terry ain't around. I guess he's not feeling so good."

What did you do, Simon asked himself almost desperately, if a man was obviously determined not to see and talk to you?

It might have been easier had Terry been his own steward, or even one on D deck; as it was, every time he attempted to see the man, he had to go up one deck; and every time one of the stewards saw him he dodged away, as if to warn Terry who was coming. Half, even three parts of all this might be imagination, but underlying it all was truth.

If he confided in the Foremans, it would be of little use, Simon decided; besides, there was no easy explanation of why he should have such keen interest in a man who had served on the *Chespeak* when he, Coll, had been a babe in arms.

The Chief Steward might help, but would need some satisfactory reason as to why a passenger should want to see one particular steward.

The truth was that he did not know how to cope with this new situation; it was of a kind he had never experienced before. The simple everyday problems of the farm and village had been taken in his stride, but this was beyond him.

It lived with him while he played deck tennis in a foursome with two bouncy, lively girls from New Jersey, and a stubby cowpuncher from Idaho.

There must be a way of explaining why he wanted to see Terry——

Ah!

*   *   *

"Good afternoon, sir." The Chief Steward's voice was pleasantly impersonal. "Can I assist you?"

"Yes, I think you can. I'd like to talk to a steward named Terry, who usually works on C deck."

"Terry, sir? That would be Terence Marchesi—I'm afraid he's sick, sir."

Simon said: "Did he really burn himself?"

"That I cannot say, sir. He reported sick this morning. Can one of the other stewards help you?"

Simon's heart began to pound.

"Well, I'm not sure. I believe that Terry served on board the *Chespeak*, about twenty-four years ago."

"That's very possible, sir."

"I would like to get in touch with anyone who served on the ship about that time," Simon said. "I think we might have some mutual friends."

"I'll have some inquiries made, sir," the Chief Steward said, formally. "And if Terry Marchesi reports for duty again, I'll have him make contact with you. It's Mr. Coll, sir, isn't it?"

"Yes," Simon said.

How did he know?

*   *   *

No one who had served on the *Chespeak* came forward, and Terry Marchesi stayed off duty. Simon said nothing about this to the Foremans, and did not go to the Chief Steward again, but half-a-dozen times he went down to C deck; the other stewards were there, but never Terry.

He found himself watching every steward on deck, in the dining-room, on the way to and from the dining-room. He didn't see Terry again, but he could imagine the man vividly—as he could picture that hawk-faced Laughing Water Smith whom he had never seen at all. By the end of the sixth day, he felt sure that he would not see the steward on board; and he gave up all hope of finding out if Terry Marchesi had been on the ship on the visit to Southampton when the hit and run accident had started that long, weary period of paralysis for his aunt—which, in the end, had killed her.

He lost a little of his tension on the boisterous final night, in the growing excitement.

A change seemed to come over everyone on board; a new mood ran through them. Women talked volubly, the souvenir counter at the shop was crowded, men gathered in slap-happy groups, in the deep satisfaction of home-coming.

Simon stood on deck next morning as the ship swung slowly round the tip of Manhattan, and the first sight of the skyline drew every feeling out of him, except great wonder; Terry Marchesi, Laughing Water Smith, Aunt Martha, all the past seemed to be struck out of his mind. People whom he had met casually on the trip waved to him, some spoke, but practically everyone was most interested in craning his neck to get a better view of Manhattan or the Statue of Liberty. Simon sensed not only their emotion, but felt some share of it, for gradually Aunt Martha's interest in America thrust itself back into his consciousness.

* * *

The sense of unreality remained with Simon as he went down the ship's gangway. In front of him in the huge customs shed was a horde of moving people, some opening trunks and cases on the floor, some impatient, some angry. The exalted mood of the deck had gone.

"As soon as all your baggage is off, sir, you join that line there, and get yourself a customs officer," a man said. Simon looked round to see the dark face of the steward who had asked Terry if he had seen a ghost. "Don't wait any longer than it takes you to make sure all your baggage is off."

"I won't," Simon said. "Thank you."

"You're surely welcome," the steward said, and turned to deal with another passenger.

Simon saw the letters of the alphabet hanging down from the roof of the shed, found a blue C, for Cabin Class passengers whose surname initial was C, looked for his cases and found them. He joined the line of people waiting at the desk, handed in his ticket, and was taken back to his baggage with a customs officer.

"Is that all your baggage, sir?"

"Just these three pieces," Simon said.

"Will you open each one, please?"

The examination took three minutes, before the officer stuck labels on to the cases and the strap of the hold-all. A porter heaved them on to a truck.

"He'll meet you at the far end of the shed, sir."

"Thanks."

The din was now worse than it had been before; there was a constant shuffle of movement and a ceaseless babble of voices. Simon reached the end of a shed, saw daylight beyond, and saw three members of the crew moving towards a door marked: *Crew*.

Simon rejoined his porter, slung the hold-all over his shoulder, picked up a case in each hand, and walked slowly towards the exit. The atmosphere was bewilderingly strange, and yet there was something that he wanted to do much more than gape. He saw a line of taxis all bright yellow, at least thirty people waiting, and almost as many porters.

Huge trucks, bigger than he had ever seen, roared and rumbled over cobbled road. Between them he could see the men coming away from the *Crew* exit of the big shed, each with some odd piece of baggage. He glanced across the wide road, pushed open the door of a snack bar, and stepped inside. A big gawkish man in shirt sleeves and braces adorned with nude women, looked up from wiping a plate.

"What's yours?"

Simon said: "I wonder if I may leave my luggage for a half-an-hour or so?"

"*What's* that?"

"Der guy wants to leave his baggage with you," honked a man further along the counter.

"Oh, sure," said the gawkish man with the braces. "That's okay. Sure, right there will do." He watched as Simon pushed the cases against a side wall.

During this brief exchange, Simon had had his back to the road for several minutes; he now realised that during that time he might have missed Steward Terry Marchesi. He walked up and down opposite the *Crew* exit, spirits drooping, deafened by thunderous lorries, which he now understood were to be called trucks. He had probably missed Marchesi. He saw Josh and Clara Foreman getting into a taxi; they had given him their address, and urged him to visit them if he travelled South.

Then he saw Marchesi.

The man carried one suitcase, and walked with the swift gait of a man in a hurry. Simon kept pace with him. Then Terry Marchesi stopped, waited, and crossed the road with a green light. He hadn't seen Simon. Simon pressed back against the window of an empty shop until the steward reached the pavement. Then he lengthened his stride.

"Terry," he said, "can I have a word with you?"

The steward swung round, startled into flinging his free arm up. When he saw who it was, the expression in his eyes changed, and the light in them seemed to glaze over. He drew in a sharp breath, hesitated for a long time, and then said roughly:

"I've got nothing to say to you. Don't bother me."

He swung round and began to hurry away, pace quickening, suitcase swaying awkwardly at his side.

Chapter 7

VIOLENCE

Simon stood watching the steward's rapid retreat. There was something disturbing in Terry's urgency. A big yellow taxi went bouncing along the cobbles, and with his free hand Terry waved to it; it swayed past him.

Simon began to walk after the steward with long, raking strides; he could overtake the man in two or three minutes, and wanted to make sure that he could not get into a rescuing taxi. He mustn't get away. Simon saw a red light at a corner, and traffic coming fast. He broke into a run. Terry stepped into the road, and a car horn screeched wild warning. He jumped back, dropping his case. Simon drew level with him.

"I want to talk to you, Terry," Simon said. "It's worth five pounds."

"Don't bother me," Terry said. There was a vicious note in his voice, a glint in his eyes which hadn't been there before. "Get to hell out of it."

"I won't keep you long, if——"

"I told you to get to hell out of it!" Terry said, his lips turned back over strong, very white teeth. "You don't mean a thing to me."

Suddenly, angrily, Simon said:

"Well, you mean a lot to me. Did you drive the car which killed Martha——"

He broke off as the other clenched his fists. He felt the raw jolt of knuckles on the side of his jaw. Pain tore at him. He saw Terry's eyes, a brown blaze of anger and fear. Simon struck the flailing arms aside. Terry backed a pace, then kicked out.

Simon staggered across the kerb, and pitched into the road. He heard a car horn screech, heard squealing brakes, as he crashed to the ground. The monstrous front of a car seemed to be inches from him.

He resigned himself to accept the impact, then the car passed, brakes and tyres still screeching. He tried to get himself to his feet, but could not. No one came to help him. He saw the back of the car which had nearly run him down, only a few yards away. Its door opened, and the driver got out—a fat man with a cigar

41

jutting straight from a big, loose, quivering mouth. The figure was grotesquely vivid. A woman appeared, and said something; then Simon felt her hands on him—feeling arms, legs, chest.

"I'm all right," he muttered. "I'm all right." He tried again to struggle up, but would not have been able to make it without the woman's help.

"He hurt bad?" That was the fat man.

"He says he's okay."

"He want to die young?"

"There was a fight."

"That so? Why'd he pick on me?"

Simon said: "I'm sorry." He was bending forward, to ease the pain, and it was going gradually, replaced by a dull ache through his whole body. "I'm sorry," he repeated lamely. It was no use explaining that he was a stranger in New York; it was no use saying anything. He had lost Marchesi. He stared along the wide street which seemed to stretch an illimitable distance away.

"I didn't knock the guy down," the fat man said, anxiously. "I didn't touch him. You know that. You don't want to report this to the cops. I didn't knock him down. He fell down himself. You saw that."

Simon said: "Please don't bother. I'm all right." He pressed his hand against his forehead. "Which way—which way is it to the docks?"

The fat man laughed, with relief as much as merriment.

"Which docks, mister?"

"There are docks stretching for three or four miles along the Hudson," the woman said.

Simon saw that other people had gathered near.

"Where the—where the United States line docks," he said.

"That's easy," the fat man said. "That way." He jerked his thumb. "Look, I got important business. You okay?"

"Yes. Thank you."

The woman said: "The guy you tangled with, he got into a taxi."

"Oh," Simon said. A wave of hopelessness, nausea and disappointment swept over him. "Yes, I—never mind. Thank you very much for your help."

"What you want is a cup of coffee," the woman said.

"Yes. Yes, I'll get one."

He turned and walked back the way he had come, stepping out more briskly as the nausea eased. He did not know how long it took him, but it seemed hours while the hot sun burned down on

42

his bare head. Then he saw the café where he had left his luggage. He went in, and the gawkish man in the bawdy braces gave him a long, raking look.

"You want something else?"

"Is there—a cloakroom?"

"Cloakroom?"

"Somewhere I can wash."

"Oh, you mean the men's room," the man said, in triumph. Others were staring at Simon, but no one made any comment. "Sure we have—that way." He pointed.

Simon saw the word *Men* on a narrow door. There was a wash basin and paper towels. His head throbbed and beat when he bent down, but after a refreshing sluice of water he felt better. Only a bruise on his forehead was left as evidence of his encounter.

He went back into the diner itself, and ordered coffee.

It was hot, and very good, sending first pain, then comfort, through his body. He sat for perhaps ten minutes, and then saw someone standing outside staring at him. He could not see the man properly because of the bright sunlight on his face, but realised that the skin was coloured. He had become used to coloured men on board the ship, among the crew; they were no longer strange. Then he saw that it was the soft-voiced steward from C deck. He beckoned. The steward hesitated, then came in. As he passed the man at the bar, he said:

"Cawfee, sir, please." He stood looking down at Simon, frowning.

"Sit down," Simon said.

"Thank you, sir. Are you okay?" The man slid into the seat opposite Simon.

Simon said: "I'm fine. Can you tell me why Terry Marchesi wouldn't talk to me?"

The coloured man said: "Can't tell you much, Mr. Coll, but you're welcome to it."

Simon said: "Thanks," and waited. The big man put the coffee in front of the steward, and disappeared.

The coloured steward said: "I can tell you this about Marchesi, Mr. Coll—he was scared bad. Yes, sir. He saw you and it was like he saw a ghost—and that ghost sure scared the pants off him."

"Did he say why?"

"No, sir," said the coloured steward. "He didn't explain a single thing. We asked him, being mighty curious, but he wouldn't say a word. He arranged with the Chief Steward to be transferred

43

to First Class, so that he wouldn't run into you, he was that scared."

Simon remembered the older man's frightened face, and the ferocity of his attack—a ferocity so clearly born of fear. It made no sense to him, but it was real enough, vivid enough, to have made sense to Terry.

"Do you know where Marchesi lives?"

"No, sir," the steward said. "I don't believe he lives in any one place, but mostly in a rooming house or a hotel. You sure don't find Terry in any one place for long. But I can tell you one thing for sure, Mr. Coll."

"And what is that?"

The dark eyes regarded him solemnly.

"Mr. Coll, I'm not a greedy man, no sir. I hope that all my friends will agree that I'm not a greedy man, but how much is it worth for you to know this information, Mr. Coll?"

Of course, he was asking for money. His information might be worth a great deal, Simon realised, but on the other hand, it might be worth nothing at all.

He said, coolly: "Ten dollars."

"Mr. Coll, you sure been to a lot of trouble to try to find out a thing which is worth only ten dollars!"

"Yes," Simon said. "Haven't I?" He finished his second cup of coffee. "Ten dollars is my limit," he went on clearly.

The steward said: "It's not enough, Mr. Coll."

"Then I'll have to find someone who can give the information to me cheaper," Simon said. He could not be sure that he was doing the right thing, but stood up, and went to the bawdy braces further along the counter. He put a dollar bill on the counter. "Take for three coffees, please."

"That guy your guest?"

"Yes."

"Okay," the man said, and pushed half a dollar and a nickel towards him.

Simon picked up the half dollar, dropped it into his pocket, and went to his cases, still where he had left them. He had one in his hand, and the hold-all over his shoulder, when the steward called:

"Mr. Coll."

Simon waited for him. He came up, teeth very bright in a wide smile.

"Like I told you, I'm not a greedy man. For fifteen dollars I'll tell you what I know."

44

Simon hesitated, then taking out his wallet, selected three five-dollar bills and handed them over.

"Thank you, sir," said the steward, "and now I can tell you this, Mr. Coll. Marchesi said you were like a man he knew on a naval cruiser—the *Chespeak*, Mr. Coll. He said it was like seeing a dead man come to life."

Simon felt a curious kind of shock. 'A dead man come to life' meant simply, harshly, that he, Simon Coll, was the living image of a man whom Marchesi had known, and who was dead.

"Are you feeling okay, Mr. Coll?" The steward was anxious.

"Yes," Simon said with an effort. "Yes, I'm all right. How long have you been on the *New States*?"

"Seven and a half years, sir."

"And Marchesi?"

"Ten years."

Simon said: "Were you and Marchesi on board on the voyage to Southampton on the last day in February?"

"Sure, it was a very rough trip," the steward said, thoughtfully. "Yes, sir."

"You're sure Marchesi was on board?"

"Yes, sir, Terry and me had our vacation around Christmas and New Year; we were both on board that trip."

Simon felt as if he was suffocating, as he said:

"Did Terry go ashore at Southampton?"

"I believe he did, sir. We were an extra day turning round that trip, because of the storm damage, and Terry went ashore. Why, he came back late!" The dark eyes lit up. "He got back so late we made a joke about it."

* * *

Of course there was still doubt, Simon knew, but all things put together seemed too much for coincidence. For a few minutes there was silence between them; then the steward said awkwardly:

"There was another thing, Mr. Coll. That night Marchesi saw you, he went along to the Radio Officer and sent a radio-telegram. I don't know who he sent it to, Mr. Coll, but he sent an urgent message to someone."

Simon asked tensely: "About me? Are you sure it was about me?"

"No, sir, I'm not sure of anything, but I can use my head," the steward answered. "Also, I can tell you the name of the Radio Officer who sent that message off—it was Mr. Matthew Geness.

45

And it just so happens I know where Mr. Geness lives, Mr. Coll."

Simon said: "Where?" and then wondered if he were going to be asked for more money. The smile faded out of the bright eyes and the big dark face was solemn for a moment; then the answer came, promptly enough.

"He lives at Baldwin, Long Island, Mr. Coll. I don't know the name of the street or the number of the house, but I'm quite sure it's Baldwin, Long Island. And he will be going home today and coming back tomorrow. The ship has a two day turn around on this trip."

The words seemed to brand themselves into Simon's mind.

"Thank you very much. Geness, Baldwin, Long Island."

"That's right," said the steward. "And I hope you find out all you want to, Mr. Coll."

He turned and walked out to the wide, cobbled road.

Chapter 8

RADIO-TELEGRAM

Simon stepped down from the train at Baldwin to an atmosphere of torrid heat. The sun was glittering on the tops of hundreds of parked cars reflecting the fierce rays.

A taxi moved up to him and he jumped in.

"Twenty-seven Fortless Avenue. Do you know it?" Simon hoped that the address in the telephone book was not an old one.

"Sure, I know it." The driver started off. "You from England?"

"Yes, that's right."

"Guess you never get anything like this in England. One hundred it will reach today, but it ain't only the heat, it's the humidity. Eighty-seven, the humidity. How about that? It makes you like being in a steam bath all the time."

The driver drove as if he was on a race track; the bright, dazzling road seemed to come up to meet him. They turned into a narrow, tree-lined street offering coolness and shadow, with small wooden houses, green lawns, and shallow white fences it was easy to step over. Outside Number 27, the driver stopped. Simon paid him rather awkwardly, and stepped towards the house.

A small child was standing beneath a lawn sprinkler, face up-turned, arms widespread, expression angelic beneath the cooling spits of spray.

A man and a woman were standing in the shadow of the house, watching the child. The man had his arm round the woman's waist. Simon recognised him as one of the officers on the *S.S. New States.*

He turned back, feeling a little guilty, and reached the front of the house. He rang the bell, and waited patiently. He rang again, before footsteps came inside and the door opened. The same woman he had seen on the lawn smiled inquiringly at him.

"Can I help you?"

"Is Mr. Geness in, please?"

"Surely," the woman said, and her eyes kindled with interest. "Who is it wants him?"

"My name is Simon Coll, and I was a passenger on the *New States,* which berthed today," Simon said. "I would be very grateful for a word with him. I won't keep him long."

"Why, that's quite all right," the woman said. She had a drawling voice, holding a hint of laughter. "Do come in and wait for him, he won't be long." She stood aside, and Simon stepped into a blessed coolness. He heard her footsteps retreat, and then a voice spoke from the doorway.

"Mr. Coll?" Geness stood there, pleasant, impersonal, his eyes a steady grey. "I hope you haven't come to me to complain about the trip!"

"It was a very good trip," Simon said. "I thoroughly enjoyed it, but——" He hesitated as Mrs. Geness came in, carrying a tray, on which were several cans of beer.

"I guess you're thirsty," she said hospitably. "In this heat who wouldn't be?"

"How very kind of you," Simon said. He was glad to be able to postpone the moment of questioning a little longer; but it could not be put off too long. "Mr. Geness," he said, "you'll think I've an infernal nerve, but I'm very curious about a radio-telegram that was sent off from the ship concerning me."

Geness said: "Mr. Coll, I'm with you on one thing—that certainly is infernal nerve." His eyes laughed. "Here's mud in your eye!" He drank. "I wish you'd brought some English beer with you. I keep telling Marjorie that until she's tasted English beer she doesn't know what beer is like."

"This is fine," said Simon. "It's wonderfully cool." He had never tasted beer so cold. "Mr. Geness, I apologise in advance, but that radio-telegram could be of extreme importance to me. I know that it's confidential, and I won't ask you to tell me what was in it, but will you tell me where it went?"

Geness said: "Which one?"

"The one which had my name in it."

"Are you sure there was one?"

Geness's wife said comfortably: "We're a long way from the ship right now, honey."

"You'd be further away if my name was cut off the pay-roll," Geness said. "But I needn't prevaricate, Mr. Coll."

"Was my name mentioned?"

"Yes, it was."

"Was it in a radio-telegram sent by a steward named Terry Marchesi?"

"That's your guess," Geness said.

"Can you tell me where it was sent to? What part of the United States, I mean?" Simon asked anxiously. "I know it's a big place, but it would be a help if I knew where to start searching."

Geness finished his beer, and put the glass down slowly.

"Why don't you tell me why you're so anxious to know, Mr. Coll? Maybe the States Line would allow me to give you that information."

Simon said: "It's so difficult to explain. It——"

He broke off, glancing at the woman, seeing something in her eyes and her expression which seemed to invite confidence. He had not talked of this to anyone, but now he found himself talking. He told them only a little of what he had discovered in England, just enough for them to know the heart of the problem —and he told of Aunt Martha's death. Next he explained exactly what had happened with the steward, on board ship, and in New York. The more clearly he described it, the more obvious Marchesi's guilt seemed to become.

When he finished, the woman said:

"Matt, you just have to tell Mr. Coll what was in that message."

Geness said, slowly: "I'd sure like to, but I've got to obey regulations."

"Now, Matt——"

"Honey, I know how far I can go," said Geness, "and I can't go as far as telling Simon Coll where that radio-telegram went, or to whom it was sent. But I can't prevent him or anyone else from reading magazines, and there's a man who made headlines a week or two ago, and in *Today* last week!"

"Headlines?" echoed his wife, and then quite suddenly she jumped up and ran into the other room.

Geness said: "I guess my wife isn't happy unless she's helping someone."

"It is my good fortune that that is so," Simon said.

Mrs. Geness came hurrying back, with a blue and red magazine in her hand; the familiar colours of *Today*.

"Matt, you don't mean——" She broke off.

"The man I mean rates the biggest headlines," Geness said. There was something curiously flat about his voice now. "And photographs."

He smiled up at his wife, and she looked almost bewilderedly from him to Simon, and then without a word she handed Simon the magazine. There was a photograph in colour, and clear bold text, which said:

Morrell Wins $1,000,000
Damages

It was a strong, powerful face, with deep-set, hooded eyes, nothing at all like Simon or anyone in that pattern which Joe Taggart had talked about. He opened the magazine, and found the story on Page 7. He could not hope to understand all the implications, but two facts stood out. This man, Lewis Morrell, had been libelled by a television and radio network, had sued, and won a million dollar damages. Simon glanced up quickly at the others, then read on. This was the last stage in a battle which had been going on for over two years, the final verdict of the Supreme Court. Lewis Morrell, who had received a cable about him, Simon Coll, was the richer today by a million dollars.

Simon said: "Who is this Morrell?"

"He's a real big guy," Geness answered. "He's supposed to be a good guy, and honest, too. There was some land out in Colorado and some more in Utah—valuable land. He bought it. Transa Television and Transa Radio allowed a news programme to go out on which a man insinuated that Morrell had killed, or ordered to be killed, the man who owned that land, then bought it from the man's daughter at a knock-down price. That price was ten thousand dollars. The value of the land today is so big that no one has started to count it yet. It runs into millions."

There was another picture inside—of a girl. The picture wasn't good enough to show whether she was beautiful or not, but there was character in the face, and appeal. The caption read:

Judith Raynor—At Time of Sale

Simon put the magazine down.

"Mr. Geness, I'm fresh to everything over here," he said, "and I'm fresh to you and the way you say things. Do you think that Morrell was guilty, and that he cheated this girl?"

Geness smiled.

"Me and about a hundred million others think that. The rest don't think about anything."

"But if it were true——"

"When you accuse a man of murder, or of instigating murder, you have to prove it," Geness said. He screwed up his dark eyes. "When they put that programme out, Transa let a man talk too much. Now they're poorer by a million bucks and we'll have to see more commercials to pay for it."

"Mr. Geness," Simon said, "are you quite sure that this Lewis Morrell is the man to whom that radio-telegram was sent?"

Geness said slowly: "It was a short cable, and all it said was 'The guy's aboard plenty curious'."

Simon's voice shook a little as he bent forward.

"Thank you, Mr. Geness. I can't tell you how much——"

"Shucks," said Geness, gruffly.

"Believe me, I mean it," Simon said. "And now I think I ought to go back to New York," he added. "Do you know the times of trains?"

"Just time for you to catch the next one, if we hurry," Geness said. "I'll drive you to the station. Train will be quicker than going by road, and you can read that article on the way."

"Mr. Coll," Geness's wife said, as her husband started up the car, "I hope you'll come and see us again. And I hope you'll find everything you want. I can't tell you how much I hope that."

Simon said: "You're very kind."

Geness drove up with the car, calling out: "You'll be in good time." He drove some distance in silence, and then spoke in a quiet, reflective voice: "Simon Coll, I don't know whether you know what you're taking on."

"Can you tell me?"

"I think you can add it all up as well as I can," Geness said, "and probably get the same answer. This Lewis Morrell may be everything his attorneys say he is, but you've heard the old saying, where there's smoke there's fire. A man died—in a mysterious mountain accident. His daughter was robbed of a fortune. The

50

profit in that land runs into millions of dollars—and someone is very sensitive about it. You're dealing with people who can be hard and ruthless and murderous. Maybe it would be a better idea if you didn't ever find out who your parents were, or whether your aunt was run down."

Simon sat, frowning tensely, as they turned into the station.

"What I'm telling you is that you may be heading for big trouble," Geness said. He put on the brakes sharply, leaned across, and opened Simon's door. "Take that magazine with you. It's on the seat." He led the way, hurrying, and they reached the platform as the train came to a standstill. Geness put out his hand and his grip was both firm and friendly. "Simon," he said, "there's one more thing that will interest you. It's in Albert Wegel's column in the *New York World Globe*. He says that Judith Raynor is in town. So is Morrell—at the *Waldorf-Astoria*. Maybe Judy could tell you something you'd like to know."

"Do you know where she's staying?"

"No, sir," said Geness, "but Albert Wegel knows. If you believe his column, he knows just about everything."

*   *   *

Simon stepped out of Grand Central Station into a stifling heat which almost stopped him in his tracks. It was nearly six o'clock. He stood at the corner of Forty-second Street. There was no slackening in the rush of traffic, and every other car seemed a bright red or yellow taxi. The pavements were thronged, and people seemed as brisk as if it were twenty degrees cooler. He stood on the corner, looking at a street plan of Manhattan, traced his present position, and saw that the Waldorf-Astoria Hotel where Lewis Morrell was staying, was not far away. He waited five minutes for a taxi, then began to walk.

The background of noise seemed hideously like the roar of a great animal, and for the first time since he had reached New York he thought of the gentle quiet of the countryside at home. Here was a kind of controlled bedlam.

He had no trouble finding the Waldorf-Astoria, but when he stepped into its crisp, welcome coolness, he felt overwhelmed by the size, the spaciousness and the luxury. At the reception desk, he hesitated. One of the plump, well-dressed men behind it came forward, unsmiling.

"Can I help you?"

"I want to find Mr. Lewis Morrell," Simon said.

The man's manner changed, subtly.

"Yes, sir, Mr. Morrell is staying with us. Do you have an appointment?"

"No," Simon said, and then said almost without thinking: "But he'll be expecting me."

"I'll send a boy up with you, sir—Mr. Morrell has a suite on the twenty-ninth floor. What name shall I tell Mr. Morrell's secretary, sir?"

Simon said: "Coll. Simon Coll."

"Thank you, sir. Boy——" He turned to a middle-aged man in attendance—"take Mr. Coll up to Mr. Morrell's apartment."

He turned away, and picked up a telephone. Simon was chilled by the magnificence about him: the fantastic beauty of the walls and some of the showcases, the soft seductive pile of the carpet, the near-silence, the well-dressed women. A row of lifts seemed to loom up in front of him. He stepped into one.

"Mr. Morrell," the bell boy ordered, and the elevator attendant closed the doors immediately. They were whisked up.

Stepping out on to a wide landing, Simon saw two men, standing facing him. They moved a little—moved together, so that they barred his path.

"Mr. Coll to see Mr. Morrell," the bell boy announced.

One of the men was taller than the other: tall, broad shouldered, very powerful looking; he had a small scar at the corner of his mouth, and curiously narrowed eyes. He stared at Simon so intently that he gave the impression that he did not mean to forget a single feature, a single line of his face. Then he said in a hard, flat voice:

"Mr. Morrell just left."

"You sure about that?" the bell boy asked, surprised. "I saw Mr. Morrell twenty minutes ago, he was coming up——"

"Mr. Morrell just left," the man repeated. "He won't be back in New York this trip." Now he turned his gaze on the bell boy, who swallowed convulsively, then turned to Simon.

"Mr. Morrell just left. You heard him. We'd better get going."

"Just a minute," Simon said, very slowly. "I don't believe that Mr. Morrell left, and I still want to see him."

His heart was pounding.

Chapter 9

ALBERT WEGEL

Simon sensed the bell boy's nervousness as he spoke; sensed that it was more than nervousness, it was fear. He looked into the narrowed grey eyes of the man who had told him that Morrell was out—and he looked past this man, towards the other, who had backed a pace, as if making sure that the door to the apartment was guarded. He himself felt the first twinges of fear, for he remembered what Geness had said. He did not yield, but stood squarely in front of the speaker. The bell boy said urgently:

"Mr. Coll, I must have made a mistake. I couldn't have seen Mr. Morrell."

"That's right," the big man said. "You made a mistake. Don't make any more."

"No, sir," the bell boy said, "no, Mr. Gatz." He put a hand on Simon's arm, and turned quickly, anxiously, towards the elevators.

"Son," said the man named Gatz, "no one around here wants to get hurt and that goes for you, too, I guess. Mr. Morrell is out and he ain't coming back. Now forget it."

Simon kept quite still. The second man backed closer to the door of the apartment. He was shorter but heavier than the first, and quite expressionless. Simon's impulse was to thrust himself forward and try to get at that door, but even if he got past one man he would come up against the other. The door might be locked, too. He saw the second man's hand go to the inside of his coat, as if he were feeling for a weapon, and that added to the sense of dream-like unreality. The bell boy was saying in a high, strident voice:

"You'd better come away, Mr. Coll."

Simon said: "Tell Mr. Morrell he might as well see me now as later. I'll wait downstairs until six o'clock."

He turned on his heel, feeling hot, angry and frustrated—and even more mystified. The bell boy stabbed the button of the elevator, and it arrived at once; as if the hotel staff meant to make sure that Mr. Morrell got good service. They stepped inside. The bell boy didn't speak, but he was sweating and pale. He stood aside for Simon to go out, and his words came low and indistinct:

"You won't do any good tangling with Mr. Morrell. Why don't you forget it?"

"That might be a good idea," Simon said.

He walked slowly towards the reception desk. The clerk looked at him curiously, and beckoned the bell boy, who went across. There was a quick exchange of whispered comment while both men stared at Simon as at a freak. He turned his back on them, and saw another bell boy.

"How many ways are there out of this hotel?" he inquired.

"Two main doors, sir, on Park Avenue and on Lexington. If you're waiting for a friend, the Park Avenue entrance will be the one for you, I imagine."

"Thanks," Simon said, and walked back over the plush carpet.

Now there were more men about. No one appeared to take any notice of him, but he felt more than ever that he was being watched. At six o'clock, he stepped out into the street, and walked to the nearest corner, where a crowd was waiting at the traffic lights. The snarl of traffic and the smell of petrol fumes on the moist air was sickening—but nothing sickened him like the rebuff he had just received, and the feeling of fear which it left with him.

He walked across with the crowd. On the other side he stepped into a shop doorway, and watched the hotel entrance; no one he recognised appeared. He waited for half-an-hour, until his feet began to ache, and the pain crept up his legs behind the knees. He wondered if he were making an absolute fool of himself.

Morrell might actually have left the hotel.

Then he saw the tall man who had stood in his way upstairs, heading for a black Cadillac. The doorman appeared, another man, and a third who was nearly as tall as Gatz; unmistakably the man of the photograph in *Today*.

So Lewis Morrell had been there but had refused to see him.

There was no hope of getting a taxi quickly; no hope of following the Cadillac. The three men got in, and the car slid off into a moving stream of traffic. Simon watched it out of sight, then walked towards Lexington Avenue, where he had passed a number of cafés and restaurants. He was hungry, he was anxious —and all he could really think about was Lewis Morrell. It had not been until the man himself had stepped into the Cadillac that Simon had really believed in him.

His concept of America had two derivations: his aunt's love of its literature and history, and the highly-coloured films and news-

aper articles depicting a tough, brutal gangster world. This
second derivation had always seemed to Simon to be touched
with the exaggeration of some of the grimmer fairy tales. He
knew that there was some truth in it, yet it was too outside his
conception of sane behaviour to be taken seriously.

Yet the behaviour of Terry Marchesi, of the men of the
Waldorf-Astoria, of Morrell being driven off in that Cadillac,
bridged the gap between the real and the half-real.

This was how gangster overlords behaved, then. It was unbelievable. Each car which passed, each tall and massive man,
reminded him of Morrell and his—legmen? Roughnecks? What
was the word?

He turned into a restaurant displaying steaks on an open
griddle in a window. Unusual food, unusual ways, kept him
occupied long enough to regain a more balanced sense of propor-
tion.

The one man who might help him was the columnist whom
Geness had mentioned, Albert Wegel of the *World Globe*.

Back in the street again, he hailed a taxi.

"Do you know the *World Globe* office?"

"Mister, I've been around this city ten years longer than the
World Globe, so if I don't, who does?"

The taxi, weaving in and out of traffic, sweeping round corners,
slid to a standstill outside a tall, grey building. A canvas porch-
way stood out halfway along the street.

Simon paid the driver, then turned to the main doors and went
in. Two peak-capped doormen stood in a vast hall of elevators.

"Do you know where I can find Mr. Wegel?"

"Seventeenth floor. They'll tell you."

As the elevator went up, Simon suddenly realised that he was
overwhelmingly tired. He hadn't given it much thought, but he
had been on the move every minute of the day, and all the time
was being driven by this fierce, unremitting compulsion.

He wondered dispiritedly whether Wegel would see him, and
whether he himself would have summoned up courage to come
this far in a Fleet Street newspaper office. The doors opened. A
girl, young enough to have retained a youthful eagerness in her
job, sat at a desk bearing the sign 'information'.

"Can I help you?"

"Is Mr. Wegel in?"

"Why, surely—but he's busy right now." She waved to a chair.
"Won't you sit down and wait?"

"Is he likely to be long?"

"You can never tell with Albert Wegel," the girl said, as if she were sharing a secret with Simon. "If you'll give me your name and tell me what you want to see him about I'll find out if he knows how long he'll be."

Simon hesitated, then said quickly: "My name is Coll. Simon Coll. I want to get in touch with Mr. Wegel about Lewis Morrell."

Immediately there was a change in the girl's expression, a quickening of interest. She lifted a telephone briskly.

"Give me Mr. Wegel." There was a short pause, and then a voice boomed. "Mr. Wegel," the girl said, "there is a Mr. Simon Coll asking for you. He would like to talk to you about Lewis Morrell." The voice boomed again. She beamed up at Simon. "Why sure I'll tell him."

Simon thought she was going to say that Wegel would not see him, but she said brightly:

"Mr. Wegel is busy right now, Mr. Coll. Could you come back in about an hour's time? He'll be glad to see you then."

An hour wasn't long and there was all New York to see—but there was also that overwhelming tiredness. Simon found himself smiling.

"Is there a waiting-room with a comfortable chair?"

"Why surely," the girl said, and smiled back. "And I can call you there when Mr. Wegel is free."

The waiting room was nearby, pleasantly filled with old-fashioned leather chairs; chairs made to accommodate the frames of tired men. Simon sat back and dozed. Time slipped by, but he had no sense of impatience or of weary waiting. It was almost with a sense of regret that he heard the telephone bell ring.

"Mr. Wegel can see you now, Mr. Coll," the receptionist said. "If you'll go along to Room 41."

He reached Room 41, a black number on a white door, and was led through an office filled with neat piles of newspapers and magazines, every shelf crammed from floor to ceiling. Another door led off this.

The fat man at the desk didn't affect him much; but at sight of the girl sitting near the window, he suppressed a sharp exclamation. It was the girl of the photograph of *Today*, the girl, Judith Raynor, who had been persuaded to sell valuable land to Morrell for a comparative song.

The fat man thrust out a short, podgy arm.

"Come in, come in," he boomed. His hand was moist but his grip was firm. "Sit down, Mr. Coll, I'm very glad to know you. This is Judy Raynor. I asked her to come and meet you. She has

an interest in Morrell, too. Very big interest, haven't you, Judy?"
He didn't give the girl time to speak but went on: "Sit down, Mr.
Coll—tell us why anyone from England would be interested in
our Mr. Morrell."

As Simon sat down, the girl looked at him intently. He wanted
to look back at her just as intently, to take in everything, to know
what she was thinking, but he felt too deep a sense of embarrass-
ment to give her anything more than a fleeting glance.

Wegel brought him back to earth as he settled into his chair,
poised, waiting.

"Take your time, take your time," he said, in a deep voice.

Very carefully, very deliberately, Simon launched into his
story. Nobody could have been more attentive than the man or
the girl. Wegel made no comment when he described his encounter with Marchesi, and his conversation with the coloured
steward. Simon went on to tell the story of his visit to the
Waldorf-Astoria. Judith Raynor did not speak, but when he told
of the threats, she put her hands to her face, as if to shut out an
ugly vision. Wegel kept absolutely still for ten or twenty seconds,
then shot out his right arm and pressed a bell push. A voice came
out of the instrument panel on his desk.

"Yes, Mr. Wegel?"

"Daisy, what plane did Morrell catch?"

"He flew out of La Guardia at seven-thirty-one, Mr. Wegel."

"Alone?"

"With Gatz. Ruff stayed behind."

"For Flagstaff, Arizona?"

"That's where their tickets took them, Mr. Wegel."

"Check that plane, check time of arrival, check Morrell
arrived on it," ordered the fat man, and flicked the instrument off.

"So he didn't want to see an Englishman who knew his dear pal
Marchesi. If you're right and he got Marchesi's radio-telegram
——" Wegel broke off, flicked the instrument on again, and the
voice came at once:

"Yes, Mr. Wegel?"

"Send a man down to Western Union. We want to try to find
out what radio-telegrams were sent from the *S.S. New States* to
Lewis Morrell this latest trip." He flicked off again and continued
almost in the same breath: "Mr. Coll, you have quite a story, you
certainly have quite a story, and I'll do all I can to find more
information for you. How much can you tell me about your
father?"

The question wrenched Simon's thoughts away from the silent Judith. She sat so still, and her eyes held—horror?

"I know nothing about my father," Simon said.

"Nothing at all?" The deep voice rose.

"Nothing at all."

"Mr. Coll," Wegel said. "I'm beginning to get more and more interested in your problem, but right now Lewis Morrell is burning up a million dollars he got out of Transa and it's my duty to make sure that he doesn't have any grounds to screw another million out of the proprietors of the *World Globe*. Do you mind having your name in my column?"

"I don't know your column," Simon said.

For the first time, the girl relaxed and gave a little laugh. The laugh was good to hear. Wegel glared at her, then at Simon, with a great pretence at severity.

"As you only arrived in New York this morning I guess you can say that and get away with it, but everybody in New York knows my column. Don't they, Judy? Everyone from the Pacific to the Atlantic and from the Gulf of Mexico to the 49th Parallel —and don't you forget it, Simon Coll. You want to know what my column is? I'll tell you. It's the most scurrilous piece of reportage outside of Hollywood. Yes, sir. Isn't that so, Judy?"

The girl said: "If you say so. All I'm sure of is that you've been wonderful to me." She meant it; she would always mean what she said, Simon thought—and then asked himself why he felt sure, why the thought even entered his head.

"Hear that, Coll?—there's a testimony for you! Now as to your story, it intrigues me, boy. It's a heart-throb story if ever I heard one. What I propose to say about you in my column is exactly this: that a young Englishman whose name we believe to be Simon Coll wanted to see Lewis Morrell and was thrown out by two muscle men."

Simon considered, and then said slowly: "I wasn't actually thrown out."

"The way you told me, you were thrown out," Wegel declared. "But all I really want to do about it is to let Morrell know that you and I have become acquainted." He laughed, as if delighted. "Okay, Mr. Coll, you're in my column, and I've known people trying for that for twenty years." He stretched out a hand for a newspaper and tossed it to Simon. "Page 21," he said.

Simon picked up the paper—and then his finger tightened on it. He stared down at a photograph of a man, whose eyes were closed but who was certainly not asleep. He stared at it for a long time, oblivious of the others, until Wegel said in a voice sharp with rising anxiety:

"What's eating you, Coll?"

The girl grew tense again, too—tense and anxious. Of course, she was afraid. She was living with fear.

Simon said: "This photograph. It's of the steward, Terry Marchesi." He began to read the brief story beneath the photograph.

"That's a guy who was run down by a hit and run car and killed in Park Avenue up at 120th Street, less than four hours ago," Wegel said. "That's how quick the *World Globe* is with the news." He sounded shaken. "Are you sure about this?"

"I haven't any doubt at all," Simon said.

Judith Raynor said, in a faraway voice: "Oh, no!"

"So Marchesi won't ever tell his side of the story," Wegel said.

Chapter 10

AXE

"All right, all right, so Marchesi's dead and can't talk, and you haven't any doubt about that," Wegel said. "And no one has any proof, either." He rubbed one of his chins, and wedged himself more firmly into his chair. His eyes seemed lost in the layers of fat when he closed them. Judith Raynor shifted her position but didn't move again. She was staring now at the columnist, that little Buddha of a man, and her hands were vice-like on the arms of her chair, as if she dared not relax her grip. "But we've lots of indications, and the most important is that Morrell was so anxious not to see you. You'd think a fine, upstanding, righteous man like Morrell would be anxious to set your mind at rest, wouldn't you? Instead, the moment he heard you were on the way to see him, he went into a panic. Judy, how about that?"

"It would take a lot to make him panic," Judith said in a low-pitched voice.

"It would take an earthquake, or a shock he wasn't prepared for. Let's work it out—and Simon Coll, let me tell you that if anyone in this world knows how Morrell's mind works, I do. I've been majoring in that subject for over a year. Now, let's see." He leaned back and clasped his hands behind his head. "It's possible that he had reason to want Martha Tenby dead, and gave the job to Terry Marchesi. It's also possible that Marchesi fixed it, and life went back to normal, until Marchesi sent that cable saying you were on the way, asking questions. Then Marchesi cabled him from New York and told him about you—so Morrell put a finger on the steward, so that he couldn't talk to you or anyone. Morrell would think he was sitting pretty—yes, sir, he would feel that his troubles were over. And then——" Wegel snatched his hands from the back of his head and slapped them vigorously on the desk. "And then the earthquake happened. Name of Simon Coll. When Morrell thought everything was calm and trouble free —Ker-rash! He must have taken it for granted that Marchesi had named him. Where else would you have got his name from?"

Wegel paused. Simon said in a husky voice:

"Nowhere."

"You bet your life—the answer was nowhere. And Morrell went into a panic. That's his one big weakness—panic reaction to bad news. When he gives himself time to think he's okay, but when you paid him a visit he could think only of one thing: keeping you away." After a short silence, he went on: "Coll, will you do something for me? Will you take Judy out to dinner? I was going to take her, she was going to tell me a lot of things I didn't know. Now she can tell you, while I talk to the City Editor and try to find out more about this accident. Like your Aunt Martha's."

Simon stood up. "I'll be very glad to take Miss Raynor out to dinner."

"So that's settled," Wegel said. "Judy, why don't you go on to your hotel and wait for me there? I'll be around by half-past ten. Okay with you?"

"Yes, of course," Judith Raynor said.

Simon said: "I'll wait with her," and they turned towards the door.

Simon opened it; Judith was about to step outside when Wegel roared:

"Hey!"

They turned round.

"Be careful," the columnist said roughly. "We don't want any more accidents."

Simon went out with the girl and they walked towards the elevator. It took them down to the ground floor and they stepped out into near darkness. The girl turned left, and Simon saw that they were on Third Avenue and 31st Street. It meant very little to him.

"My father was also killed in an accident," Judith said. "In a rock fall."

"So I read."

There was nothing else to say.

"They called it an accident," Judith went on. She looked up at Simon. The sadness remained in her expression, and yet could not take away the kind of beauty which was hers—not the arresting beauty of stage or studio, but one quiet and glowing, touched by hidden fear. "Where are you staying?"

"I put my bags at Grand Central Station," Simon answered. "I haven't booked in at a hotel."

"There'll be room at mine," Judith said. "The Five Star at 40th and Seventh. It's on the other side of the town," she explained. "We ought to get a taxi." She looked along the wide avenue. "There's one," she said. She raised her hand, but the driver didn't see her.

"Taxi!" Simon shouted, and stepped into the road, Judith beside him.

Almost on that instant a taxi started up, and came hurtling towards them. With a biting spasm of fear, Simon saw the way the driver crouched over the wheel. In an instant he swept the girl up and leapt for the sidewalk. The taxi hurled itself over the kerb, and for a moment it looked as if it could not miss them. Simon felt the blast as it tore past, regained the roadway, and raced on. He stood with one arm tightly round Judith Raynor, her face pressed against his chest. He had a swift and fleeting vision of another moment when a woman's body had been close against his, and wished from the bottom of his heart it had never happened.

"Let's go," he said in a gruff voice, letting his arms drop to his sides.

A taxi slid past and stopped at the entrance to a nearby building. As the passenger got out, the taxi sign lighted up again.

"This one's bound to be all right," Simon said. He helped the girl in, aware of her long, lovely legs. She dropped down into the corner, and sat staring ahead. "The Five Star Hotel," Simon ordered and the driver started off, without a word. He didn't speak until they were in the middle of the thick traffic. Suddenly, on his right, he saw a street of lights so bright it was hard to believe that there could be so much brilliance in one place. It jolted him out of the mood of shock and alarm and transition,

61

and he asked in a wondering voice: "Where's that?"

"Why, that's Times Square," Judith answered. "Haven't you seen it before?"

He shook his head, smiling.

"I wish I never had. I think I would give every dollar in the bank to be back in Red Rock." Her voice became harsh and dry in that moment. "I don't know about you," she went on, "but I'm terrified."

"Me, too," Simon said. The taxi turned a corner, the bright lights were cut off, and he was thrown against the girl. "I know what you mean. Is Red Rock your home?"

"I spent most of my life there. I wish I had never gone away."

She was dry-eyed, and yet she had a look of infinite grief, of deep and lasting sorrow. The taxi drew up. Simon handed the fare over the front seat, stepped out, then followed the girl into the hotel.

He saw a passage connecting two halls, and an open door at the far end. He took her arm again, and walked her through towards the other street.

"Judy," he said, "I think you ought to change your hotel. I don't think it's safe to be where everybody knows you're staying."

Now that he had said this, he felt that he was right; but it had come into his mind swiftly and unbidden, without thought. Judith's step checked for a moment, as she stared at him. This was the first time he had been able to look at her clearly and in a good light.

She was tall for a woman, five eight or so, with blue-grey eyes, wide-set, and very clear. She had a short, straight nose, and a mouth that would, under happier circumstances, perhaps, have smiled often.

She said in a voice she was striving to keep practical: "Wegel will be calling here."

"We can telephone his office and tell him we'll be somewhere else," replied Simon. "I can still feel the wind of that taxi."

"I know," she said. "Like the breath of death."

"Do you know of another hotel?"

"Well," she said, "my father always stayed at the Dorset. It's up town——"

Simon said: "I don't think you ought to be where your father always stayed."

He was aware of his own heightened sensitivity to danger, and surprised by it; it was as if a part of his mind, closed until now, had opened suddenly.

"Let's get out of here," he said. "We'll take a taxi, go find a hotel, and then come back for your baggage."

"It won't take me twenty minutes to pack," Judith declared. "I can check out when I've finished, and I'll feel much safer."

"Then why don't we do that?" Simon said.

They went up to the seventeenth floor, and stepped out along the corridor. The day had been a succession of unfamiliar scenes, unfamiliar passages, moving doors, swift movement, with a strangeness which seemed to become familiar as only minutes passed. Judith took out her key. He took it from her, thrust it in the lock and threw the door open. The first glimpse of the room told him that something was badly wrong.

"What is it?" Judith asked, and looked over his shoulder.

The room was a chaos of torn and savagely ripped clothes. A handbag had been turned inside out, and its lining ripped away. None of the hotel property seemed to have been damaged, but powder, lipstick and nail varnish had been emptied over the dressing table. The bathroom door stood wide open, and tooth-paste had been trampled over the tiles; all the toilet oddments were broken.

Simon turned to look at Judith. She had lost all colour, and her eyes were bright with fear. Suddenly she moved towards the bed, pulled up the mattress, and looked underneath. She let the corner fall heavily.

"I had two hundred dollars there. It's all gone." She looked round the wrecked room, and he was prepared for her to burst out crying, or to rave with anger at the damage. Instead she said: "Well, I guess I haven't anything to pack." She started for the door with quick, nervous movements, but as she did so, the telephone bell rang.

Simon stepped past her, saying: "I'll answer it."

She didn't protest. He wondered if it could be Wegel, but was not surprised when a man's voice said brusquely:

"Tell Judy Raynor to go back home or she'll run into serious trouble."

"Who——" Simon began.

"And that goes for you too," the man said.

He rang off.

Chapter 11

BIRTH OF CUNNING

Judith was standing with her back to the door.

Two men walked along in the passage.

"*. . . and I told him, if you'd come to see me first you could have made another hundred dollars. Jack, I told him . . .*"

Judith moved back with one arm outstretched behind her, touched the door, and closed it. She stood quite still, as if waiting for fear to drain out of her. When she spoke it was in a low-pitched voice, but it had all the cadence which Simon had noticed earlier.

"What did the man say?" she asked.

"He told us to go back home," answered Simon, and after a pause, he asked: "Has he talked to you before?" He felt sure that he knew the answer before she said:

"Yes."

"How often?"

"Two or three times."

"Have you told Wegel?"

She shook her head.

"Why not?"

"Because he would have told the police."

"Wouldn't that be the wise thing?"

"I don't think so."

"Why not?"

"I don't believe the police would believe me."

He looked round the room, and waved.

"They would have to believe this."

"No," Judith said. "They wouldn't have to believe it. It's perfectly possible to theorise that I'd done all this myself. They already think I'm a little mad. They're very kind about it, but they think I'm mad because I was so fond of my father, and his death turned my head. That's reasonable, too."

"They wouldn't imagine that man's voice on the telephone," Simon said. "I heard it."

She gave an amused smile—the kind of smile which said: *I've heard all this before*.

"I've got friends, haven't I? Those friends could telephone, knowing you were here." She came forward slowly, and Simon was strangely aware of her grace of movement. "Simon," she said, "there's just one man left in New York who believes I am as sane as he is—the trouble is, a lot of people believe that he's mad, too."

"Albert Wegel?"

"Yes."

Simon hesitated, choosing his words with care.

"Judith, have I got this situation right? You've been threatened several times and told to leave New York?"

"I've been told to stop seeing Wegel," she corrected. "He's the man who worries them, because of his column. His column did more harm to Lewis Morrell than the defending attorney. That's why they want me away from New York. They can handle me in Red Rock."

"Handle you?"

"Keep me quiet."

"And you don't want to be kept quiet?"

"No," said Judith. "No, I don't want to keep quiet. but sometimes I think they'll make me. All this has been going on for such a long, long time." She looked overwhelmingly tired, as she stooped to pick up a dress which had been slashed to ribbons. She let the pale soft fabric pass through her fingers, time and time again, as she continued to speak. "It's been more than a year now. I can't fight for ever. I don't think anyone else would have fought as long as Wegel." Her voice dropped to a whisper. "After a year, a remembered scene becomes vague. Things which were once vivid and clear begin to fade. Even my father's face— sometimes I can hardly remember what he looked like. I am no longer certain whether I've been fighting for him all this time, or whether I'm fighting because I got hurt, and want to hit back."

"I think I know what you mean," Simon said. He ran his hand across his forehead, and gave a little shiver. "Judith," he repeated, "I'm going on looking for my father, for the answer to all the questions. I have to. And I've been thinking——"

A thought had flashed into his mind, vanished, and come back; his mind twisted and turned in a desperate endeavour to assess the situation and decide what to do.

Judith looked at him inquiringly.

"Tell me."

"I've been thinking that it might be a good idea if we allowed Morrell to believe that we've been frightened off."

"I don't understand you."

"Does Morrell spend a lot of his time near your home?"

"Yes—there and in San Francisco."

"Where is Red Rock?"

"In Southern Utah," she answered slowly. "It's a little town way out in the desert. The mining is done in the mountains near."

"Mining?"

She said: "They found gold. My father prospected the Red Rock country all his life, and he believed the gold was there. After he died they found it in big veins close to the surface. The ore is carried by truck to the railroad and the crushing and refining plant. Morrell has built himself a big house in the mountains nearby. That's where he lives much of the time."

"Just gold," Simon said heavily.

"If there's enough of it, that's plenty."

"Oh, yes," Simon agreed, "but in your situation I think I'd give up."

She began to play with the fabric again, and it was a long time before she answered.

"It's no use," she said at last. "I can't do it. A hundred times I've told myself I would have to, but I can't. I think Morrell killed my father, and while I have any hope of proving it I have to go on." She raised her head and looked at him straightly, wearily. "I don't want to. Most of the time, I resent the urge to keep on fighting. I could live a very happy life. My father has been dead for over a year, and I could live happily at Red Rock, but I just have to go on." She stopped, frowned as if at some vivid memory, and went on: "Do you ever feel like that?"

"Just like that," Simon said. It was strange and good to hear someone express his own feelings so clearly. "That's what's been on my mind, that's why I'm here. Can you find the proof you want at Red Rock?"

"If I can find it anywhere, it will be there," she said. "My father went into the mountains with an old friend. He sent his friend back with a message; he had seen men working on land he worked and wanted the State Police to know. The lease to work that part of the mountains came from his agreement with the Nhovi Indians. He knew the Nhovis well, and worked with them for years. Other prospectors often tried to jump Nhovi claims, that was why they leased everything to my father. He would sub-lease to anyone with genuine claims, and all the gold found was divided with the Nhovis."

"Is Morrell sharing his finds with them?"

"No—he pays them a nominal sum, nothing like as much as it

66

should be—and many of the big lodes are just beyond the boundaries of the reserve. My father died near one of these lodes," Judith went on. "When the police arrived they found him buried under tons of rock—the rock he loved." The girl broke off, and her eyes lost their clearness and became misted over. "We don't know whom he saw or what he saw after his friend had gone. If I could make Morrell talk——" She broke off.

"If I can find out what I want to know, I'll find it from Morrell," Simon said. "And so can you."

The telephone bell rang again. Simon stopped speaking to stare at it. Judith was nearer, but didn't stretch out her hand. There was another long peal, and Simon could imagine that rough menacing voice of the man he had heard before. The bell rang for a third time. Simon lifted the receiver.

"Hallo?"

"Is that you, Simon Coll?" Although the man's voice was deep there was no hint of menace. Simon mouthed to Judith: "It's Wegel," then spoke into the receiver.

"Yes, Simon Coll here."

"Simon," said Wegel, "I've news for you, bad news. You aren't going to get your name in my column. Nor is Judith. The *Globe World* has finished with the Morrell case. My boss has spoken. The decision of the Supreme Court shall be taken as final and binding, and anything more I write about it could be held as contempt—and might see me on the breadline. Of course, I could hand in my resignation. I could say shucks to the *Globe World* and get another job, but I don't know of another newspaper owner who would pay me half as much as my present boss, and I always liked money. Will you tell Judith?"

Simon said: "As you say."

"Hey, there!" Wegel cried. "Hold on a minute. You remember telling me that the Southampton police checked with the States Line—about that accident to your aunt?"

"Yes," Simon said, breathlessly.

"I've just heard from a friend at Police Headquarters," Wegel said. "There was an inquiry from Southampton about fingerprints found on the wheel of the car which knocked Martha Tenby down."

"Well?"

"The prints were Marchesi's," Wegel said, simply. "He died the way your aunt was killed. The police are after the car which ran him down, but——" He broke off.

Simon said: "And in spite of this, you're backing down?"

"I'm doing what my boss tells me," Wegel retorted. "You make sure Judith knows that."

Simon rang off, and turned to face Judith. He could hardly keep his voice steady, the positive news about Marchesi was so devastating and conclusive. Now it was not a simple case of guesswork and theory; he had absolute facts to go on.

"He's dropping the case from his column," he told Judith at last, and added almost savagely: "Now and for ever—until we prove you're right about Morrell. And you're certainly right. Marchesi . . ."

She made no comment when he finished telling her.

"Judith, we've got to prove him wrong."

"It isn't Wegel's fault," she said at last. "He told me a week ago that if Morrell won this appeal to the Supreme Court, the newspaper would probably drop it."

"That leaves the two of us and a certainty," Simon said. He had to go on as if taking her agreement for granted, but could she feel as positive as he? Aunt Martha was only a name to her. "Two of us—against how many?" he made himself ask.

"At Red Rock alone, there must be twenty men who work for Morrell," Judith said. "Apart from those who work in the hills for his mining company." She was silent for a long time, her hands limp by her side, the only expression showed in her eyes. "Simon, I think this is the moment when I just have to say it's no use." She paused again. "Well, I have to try to say it, anyway. Without Wegel—we can't do anything at all."

"Judith," Simon said, "I've got a different thing to fight for. I can't stop."

She didn't answer.

"I don't want to involve you, and if you want to stop, I accept it as reasonable, but I have to go on." He fought against the disappointment which her words had created, and went on doggedly. It was easy to understand the turmoil in her mind, to admit that she was saying the sensible thing. No woman could go on after this. With Wegel's support she had hope, but an Englishman fresh from England could only be a liability. Yet his own compulsion had become ten times stronger because of what he now knew. "I've got to go and see Morrell. I've got to talk to him. Why don't you stay away from Red Rock until I've come back—just forget that we ever met?"

She said: "You told me you'd been thinking. How far did it get you?"

"This far," Simon answered at once. "That you should go

away for a few weeks, on a vacation. I will go on alone to Red Rock. No one will blame you for what I do. If Wegel's column has dried up, and you've left New York, why should Morrell make any more trouble for you?"

Judith didn't answer.

"I've got to look for the evidence I want. I can also look for the evidence you need. I'll be new to the country, but that may not be such a handicap."

"You would really go there alone?"

"I'm going to Red Rock to see Morrell. I have to. If he won't see me, I'm going to find out why."

"Simon——" Her voice tailed off.

"Yes?"

"They nearly killed you tonight."

"I know," Simon said. "And they nearly killed you. There are two more reasons why I want to see Morrell and the men who work for him. But he won't kill me. He won't even attempt to." The words were clear enough, but hollow even in his own mind.

"Simon, you should go to the police," Judith said. "This finger-print evidence makes a good reason."

"Does it?" Simon asked, wryly. "The man who killed Martha Tenby is dead, and the police are looking for the driver who ran him down. What more can they do?"

"You must tell them everything," Judith insisted.

"There's one snag," Simon said. "One reason why I don't want to go to the police."

"I can't imagine any good reason."

"There's this," Simon said. "I mean to go to Red Rock and see Morrell. If I go to the police with this story now, they'll keep me in New York, for questioning. They're bound to. If they know that there was an attempt to kill you and me tonight, if they know of the connection with the inquiry from the police at home, they're certain to keep me here. And I want to go after Morrell at once. He's alarmed. Wegel knows him, and Wegel says he's been panicked. I want to keep after him."

"But you can't just go to Red Rock! I don't believe you have any idea of what you're taking on. You can't have." Judith stood up and moved towards him. "You don't know the desert and you don't know the mountains. In that country a thousand men could get lost in a night. A man could disappear off the face of the earth, and no one ever find his bones again." She drew in a sharp breath.

"Judith——"

She turned passionately towards him, gripping his hands.

"I tell you you don't understand what you're saying. You can't even begin to imagine what that country is like. It's so hot that it burns you. Off the highways, where you can't get food or gas or a place to sleep, it's like it was a thousand years ago. There's nothing but rock and sand and heat. For big distances of hundreds of miles between the highways, there's no water, no food, no animals, no birds. Simon, believe me—Red Rock desert country can kill men who have lived there all their lives. And the mountains can swallow you up. It's the most beautiful country in the world, and the most dangerous unless you know your way about. You couldn't hope to find anything without a guide. I've spent my life there, and there are valleys and canyons where I won't even set foot. You can't go there alone."

She paused only for a second, as if to judge whether she was making any impression.

"Simon, you've got to understand. You mustn't go there alone. Every year a dozen or so prospectors go looking for gold and uranium, and very few of them come back. They've been toughened by years of prospecting, they know all the tricks, they go prepared for any emergency—and they still die. Believe me, you'll be throwing your life away."

"You could be right," Simon said. "But I have to try. I'm going, Judith. Can you tell me of a man who would act as my guide?"

In the long, long pause which followed, she studied him, as if trying to judge if there was any hope of changing his mind. Then she raised her hands and dropped them heavily, hopelessly.

"There's one man who might go with you. He was the friend of my father, half Nhovi Indian, half white—a man named Laughing Water Smith. The Indian names——"

She broke off, startled, at Simon's expression.

He saw that imagined picture of the man who had been in Weymouth, the man the old mayor had remembered, the man from the *Chespeak*, who was still alive. He told Judith.

"So now nothing will stop you," Judith said helplessly. "Simon, at least talk to Wegel. Ask him what he would do. He'll help if he can, I'm sure of it."

* * *

"Sure, the police would hold you," Wegel said, "and so they should. Listen, boy. I'll give you a start, and then I'll tell the police where you've gone. That way you can call on the Arizona police if you need to—they'll know all about you. And if I were you, I would talk to Johnny Rowman, of the *Unity Press Agency*. He'll run any story you send back. You arrange to report in once daily to Johnny, by telephone or telegram. If you miss a day, Johnny will start screaming—and Johnny Rowman's scream can be heard all over the U.S.A. Be sure of that, Simon. He's your man."

* * *

"Why, sure," said Johnny Rowman. "Sure. Let's do that, Mr. Coll."

Part II

THE LAND OF THE RED ROCKS

Chapter 12

WHISTLE STOP

Simon looked out of the wide window of the Pullman carriage on to great stretches of pale, rolling desert, broken only by spindly bushes.

The whole vista seemed as if it had been flung down when the earth had been created, and left to make its own ruin. Here and there silvery flowers, shimmering at the end of shoulder-high stalks, told of life. Except at or near the railway stops, he had seen no sign of habitation all that day. The train trundled on, sometimes slowly, sometimes very slowly, never as fast as he had expected.

Now, it began to pick up speed.

Two passengers passed, waving. Simon preferred to sit here, on his own. No one on the train particularly interested him, nor he them. He had never known so much to think or dream about. Into those dreams now appeared the figure of Judith Raynor. At times, her face was almost everything he saw, blotting out all other visions. Then it would fade, and that imagined picture of Laughing Water Smith would replace it; or the powerful face with the hooded eyes—Lewis Morrell. Or the hard toughness and the glinting eyes of the man Gatz.

Suddenly, he caught sight of a great high ridge of red rock, rising out of the desert like a huge man-made wall. He stared in awed fascination. In the distance he had seen ridges of such formations, but nothing so vivid as this. He caught his breath. The rock face seemed close enough for him to touch. Weird shapes stood out like the carvings of prehistoric creatures cut with sharp flints. He peered as far ahead as he could, then jumped up and hurried to the end of the carriage. He stepped out of the compartment on to the platform, and felt the blast of heat-laden air.

They were entering a great gorge, with rock on either side, rising hundreds of feet above them. Ahead it was quite dark, the sun shut right out. At the side of the track, the red dust looked as if it were several feet thick and it was impossible to believe that men had ever set foot here. The weird carvings drew nearer, and he could see the incredible intricacy of the shapes—all carved by the wind and the rain, the snows and the water of millions of years. The train rumbled slowly forward, as if its driver were afraid that he would shake down the grandeur of the centuries from the lowering sides. Simon had expected intense heat, but now that they were inside the gorge it was cooler—the air stream made by the passing of the train was almost chilly.

He heard a door close. A passenger he had seen several times spoke just behind him.

"Is this your first trip, sir?"

Simon turned his head.

"Yes, it is."

"And you like it?"

"Like it?" Simon said. "Like it?" He raised his hands helplessly. "I can't describe what it does to me."

The man was elderly, tall, with snow-white hair and a pleasant, weather-beaten face.

"Some people call it pretty, and think no more about it," he said. "Some fall in love with it at first sight, and never forget it. This is Red Devil Gorge," he added. "Beyond there to the west and north is Red Rock country."

Simon was staring out of the window, glad that his expression could not be seen.

"Red Rock country?"

"That's right," the stranger said. "The most desolate country in the whole of the United States, sir, and the most beautiful. I don't believe there is more beautiful country in the world. Behind that rock, there are tracts of land where the white man is unknown, and few Indians have ever walked. You're right in the heart of the American desert, sir, in prehistoric America."

"How far away is—Red Rock?"

"The whistle stop's at the end of the canyon," said the stranger, his voice quickening with interest. "We'll be there in about half-an-hour, I guess. Are you interested in Red Rock?"

"I'm getting off the train there."

"At Red Rock?" The man sounded incredulous.

Simon laughed.

"Is it so wild?"

"You bet it's wild," the other said, "but I wasn't thinking of that. Most people go to Little Bend, thirty miles further on, where the mining camps are."

"I'm going to Red Rock," Simon said.

"You got friends there?"

"I'm going to see an old friend of my father's."

"Is that so?" the stranger asked, curiously. "Well, sir, I know this country almost as well as I know the back of my hand. I've been coming to Red Rock and to Little Bend for the past forty years, and I can't imagine who you would be going to visit. My name is Killany, Dr. Killany. I'm glad to know you, Mr.——"

Simon said: "Coll, Simon Coll." He took the proffered hand, and was sure that the name meant nothing to the man. "Are you going to see Lewis Morrell?"

"Yes, sir," Dr. Killany said. "I'm going to spend a short vacation with him."

Simon said: "That's very interesting."

"Why don't you visit him?" Killany suggested. "I'm sure you would be very welcome."

"Perhaps I will," Simon said. "I want to see as many people as I can while I'm out here. A big newspaper in New York has asked me to report on an Englishman's reaction to this part of the United States. They'll be following my movements with great interest." He smiled. "Every day I have to send them a telegram, and if it doesn't arrive, they'll send search parties out for me. Doesn't that sound sensible to you, Killany?"

The older man looked puzzled, but he said: "Yes, yes, very sensible," and turned away.

Simon turned back to Red Devil Gorge, both awed and fascinated, and Killany said a little awkwardly:

"I hope to see you again, Mr. Coll."

"Thank you," Simon said.

He went back to his compartment, sat down, and closed his eyes. The rumble of the train told him that they were still going through the Gorge, but the great walls of mighty grandeur were further away from the track now, and the vivid red seemed to have faded a little. He felt a pulsing excitement and the chill touch of fear. Laughing Water Smith lived somewhere in the foothills of the mountains. He knew exactly where to find him, for he had spent two more days in New York, and Judith had told him all she could—about Red Rock itself, the mountains, her father, her life, her friends. He felt that he had known her all his life; far, far longer than he had ever known Dorothy.

He heard a footstep, looked round, and saw Dr. Killany.

74

"Mr. Coll."

"Yes, sir?"

"I sure hope you know where you're going to stay in Red Rock. There's no hotel there, and there may be a few cabins, but it's a pretty rough spot."

"I know where I'm going to stay," Simon said.

Killany frowned, shrugged, and went off as if puzzled. He was pleasant-voiced, had a friendly face and a friendly manner; yet Simon felt antagonised, as he would have felt by any friend of Lewis Morrell.

He saw the wall of the gorge close in again, and those writhing shapes were very close. Then quite suddenly the rocks fell away, and they were in the open desert. The whistle blew. The red cap appeared at the doorway, white toothed smile vast and delighted as if he had brought the long train here by his own unaided efforts.

"Here you are, sah—Red Rock!"

Simon said: "That's fine."

He stood up, and went to the end of the compartment. The train was slowing down. The colour of the sand here was much redder than it had been at the other end of the gorge, but the land was as flat as the eye could see except to the right, where the mountains rose in an enormous cliff. Then he saw a road, winding towards the west, coming across the desert and apparently crossing the railroad track. The whistle blew again, and the train stopped. A wooden hut stood close to the track, and a larger one fifty feet away. An old car, the cellulose burned off it to a pale grey, one tyre flat, stood bared to the vicious sunlight. The heat struck at Simon through the open door. He stepped down, and the hand rail he held was hot to touch.

No one was in sight, but some distance off there was a little cluster of wooden buildings, and the winding road which looked as if it was covered with drifting sand. Nothing stirred; here, there was no wind.

"Ain't you being met, Mr. Coll?" the red cap asked.

"No," Simon said.

He watched the man put his cases down, as puzzled as Killany had been. Several faces were pressed against the windows of the compartments, Killany's among them, but none made any attempt to come and speak. A small child waved both hands vigorously, and mouthed a message through the window, but Simon could hear no sound. The whistle blew. The red cap climbed back on to the footplate.

"Thank you, Mr. Coll. I sure enjoyed having you on board."

"I enjoyed the ride," Simon said.

He wanted to laugh, yet there was no cause for laughter. There was this fierce, driving excitement, and the spur of fear. Over there, nestled against the foothills, lived Laughing Water Smith—and a part of his own beginning. The train began to move off. His excitement almost choked him, but there was another feeling with it. It seemed as if the civilised world too, was gliding out of his life. It was a crazy thought, but on that instant he felt panic; felt that he was mad to be out here on his own. He should have listened to advice; it wasn't until this moment that he had known any real concept of the situation. The last coach passed. Already, the train began to look smaller. The track curved round in the waste of desert, the sleepers now covered with red dust—and not far along, the only sign of the track was the glistening rails themselves.

And then there came stillness and silence.

Simon looked about him. No one and nothing stirred from the two huts, one of them marked *Passengers*, the other marked *Freight*. But there had been no other passenger and no freight. He looked towards the east and north, towards the forbidding mass of the red mountains, and from here they looked even more vivid, for the sun was shining directly on them.

The cluster of buildings must be two hundred yards away. Simon saw the broken surface of the tarred road which led to them from the whistle stop, and the bleached car standing out in the frizzling heat. Then he heard a car engine start off, and saw a car moving towards him. It looked nearly as derelict as the one near him. The car rattled and shook; one of the wings seemed to be falling off. An old man was driving it, one arm out of the window, one hand negligently on the steering wheel. As he drew up, he said:

"Hey, mister, glad to see you. Nobody told me there was any passengers for Red Rock on that train. No, sir, no one told me, or I'd have been there waiting for you." He pushed open the creaking door of the car, and jumped down. He was small, wizened, pale-faced; a straw was sticking out of one side of his mouth. "That your baggage?" The old man picked the two cases up and flung them into the back of the car. "You booked to stay with Ma Neilson?"

"I don't know," Simon said. He put the hold-all in, and climbed up next to the driver.

"You telling me you don't know where you're staying? You

come prospecting?" The eyes were filled with scepticism and derision.

"Kind of," said Simon, and surprised himself by using the phrase. "I'm sorry," he said. "I'm not used to this heat. I've come to see—an old friend." He stopped at that; he did not want to say too much too soon. "Who is Mrs. Neilson?"

Ma Neilson ran the café, the only store, the gas station, and the only motel at Red Rock; six wooden cabins, part of the cluster of buildings. There was very little that Simon didn't know about the individuals who lived in and near Red Rock, for Judith had briefed him well; but he was here as a stranger, coming only to see Laughing Water Smith. "Don't talk to anyone," Judith had advised, "until you've seen Laughing Water. Especially don't talk to Ma Neilson or Andy Lapp. Andy is the gas station attendant, the taxi driver, the odd-job man in Red Rock, and it seems as if he grew up with the town."

"Sure is hot," Andy Lapp admitted. "But I tell you, I know'd it hotter, at least once. Nineteen thirty-one, yessir, you could've fried eggs on the sidewalk, and that's a fact." He cackled with laughter. "Where shall I take you? Ma Neilson's?"

"Is that the only place to stay?"

"You bet. It sure is," Andy said. "There ain't no place else."

"Then I'll be glad if you'll take me there."

The café was a low-roofed building of knotted pine. Beyond it were some outbuildings, and an old Indian, with thick, greasy, grey hair, sat cross-legged in the shade of a doorway, doing something with a needle. There was a drone of an engine, and a windmill was turning slowly. Opposite the café was the gas station; two pumps, once scarlet and now pale pink, with battered signs and hoses which were tied up with rags. Over these was a mushroom-shaped concrete roof, as if there had once been an attempt to make this place seem alive. The old man stopped outside the café, and as Simon got out, he asked:

"How much is that?"

"Gee, mister, we don't charge nothing for the ride," Andy Lapp said. "Maybe you would like to buy me a cup of cawfee." He followed Simon inside.

The contrast was startling. On one side was a clean café, with a counter, a dozen booths, bright, fresh red formica everywhere. On the other was a small market, the groceries and dry goods in rows all clearly marked; a big refrigerator at one end was humming faintly. An elderly woman was sitting at a cash desk. She looked up as Simon entered.

Simon went up to her, smiling; but he was puzzled by the woman's expression. Its blank hostility reminded him of Gatz, one of Morrell's men at the *Waldorf-Astoria*—a fantastic contrast to this desert oasis. "I would like to rent one of your cabins, for a day or two. How much will it be?"

She stared at him, then shot a glance at Andy Lapp—a glance which obviously conveyed some message.

"I'm sorry, mister, we're filled right up. Ain't got a bed in the place."

Andy's mouth opened in a gasp of incredulity. Ma Neilson glared at him, then rested a plump hand flat on the desk in front of her.

"Best thing you can do, mister, is have something to eat, and then take the Western Flyer back to Albuquerque. She's due in at nine o'clock tonight. There ain't no accommodation in Red Rock, none anywhere at all."

She was lying, of course; she had been warned to expect him and warned to turn him away.

Chapter 13

OLD MAN'S CABIN

Simon returned the woman's gaze. Andy Lapp looked away, towards the door behind the bar. A Mexican girl began to wipe off some coffee stains with a damp cloth. She stared at Simon with dark, luminous eyes, as if fascinated by a stranger, perhaps fascinated by his English accent.

"That's a pity, Mrs. Neilson," he said. "I shall have to camp out."

"You'll be a fool if you do," the woman said. "You'd best catch the Western Flyer."

"Didn't Morrell tell you what to do if I refused to catch the train?" asked Simon, and when she didn't answer, just lost a little of her colour, he went on: "I have to make a telephone call to New York. Do you have a booth here?"

She nodded.

"I have to make a call to the Unity Press Agency once every day," Simon went on. "Then they know where I am and where they can get in touch with me, and they'll contact the police if I

78

get into any trouble. They know that Red Rock mountains are dangerous."

"There's a telephone," she said. "The operator will tell you how much." She looked put-out as she moved the papers on her desk.

Simon sauntered to the counter.

"When Andy Lapp comes in, I'd like him to have a coffee with me," he said to the Mexican girl, and put fifteen cents on the counter. "Will you arrange that for me?"

"Sure, *si, si, senor*."

"Thank you." Simon went to the telephone, lifted it, dialled, and waited; when he gave his number, a girl operator said: "There will be a delay of fifteen minutes, sir." "I'll wait," said Simon, and turned back.

He stood by the window, watching a yellow truck which seemed to have appeared out of nowhere. A cloud of dust billowed up as it pulled off the road. A youth climbed down from the driving seat, long thin legs in tight-fitting jeans, hips slender as a young boy's. He leaned inside the cabin, thrusting his arms forward, and a moment later brought out a babe-in-arms; a young girl jumped down from the other side. They were laughing as they came in. The boy said: "Howdy?" Simon nodded. They ordered soda, and had started on them when the telephone bell shrilled out.

Simon answered.

"Your call to New York, Grammercy . . ." the operator said.

"Fine," Simon said, and a moment later he heard Johnny Rowman's voice.

"Simon Coll?"

"Yes, and I'm still alive," Simon said. "Although I'm having some difficulty in finding accommodation. I'm at Red Rock Railroad stop . . ." He said little enough, but knew that everyone within earshot was listening intently. He rang off, and waited for the operator to call back; the call cost a dollar-fifty. He paid Ma Neilson, and went outside, his cases were standing in the darkness of a shelter made of cactus leaves. It was a little after five o'clock, and he wasn't sure what time it got dark. He picked up the hold-all, slung it over his shoulder, and started to walk towards the foothills of the Red Mountains. He had never known such a sense of isolation; just as the train had seemed to be stranding him in the dark centuries, now he seemed to be walking away from everything he had ever known.

Nothing stirred. The heat was stifling, the bag already making a sticky patch on his back. He narrowed his eyes as he looked towards the foothills. He saw the outline of a cabin fairly high up but on the lower slopes, between two huge outcrops of rock. That was Laughing Water Smith's cabin. Judith had told him that the old sailor's home was three miles away from the railroad; three miles, in the cool of a Dorset summer, was a pleasant evening walk; three miles in this burning heat had the makings of an ordeal. The road was tarred, but there were great cracks and pot-holes in it, under a layer of the red dust.

Simon pushed his hat to the back of his head, and wiped his forehead. He heard a car or truck behind him, but did not look round. He could not be sure that, in spite of the telephone call, Morrell would not risk causing another 'accident'. His teeth set tightly, and his jaws hurt. He stepped to the side of the road. The engine rattled noisily. Then the truck drew alongside, and he glanced up to see the young couple with the child. The girl was nearest to him, the window open.

"Hi, there!" she cried, "like a ride?"

"You're surely welcome," the boy called; he was leaning over his wife's shoulder. "How far you going?"

"To Laughing Water Smith's cabin up there," Simon pointed.

"We go right past," the girl said. "You want to get in?" She opened the door, and he climbed up. There was room for him, but they were tightly packed, the baby swinging in a mobile crib, just behind them.

"You're very good."

"You're surely welcome," the youth repeated. "Mister, when we hear you say there weren't no room at Red Rock we began to wonder if you'd heared aright. There ain't no more than two of Ma Neilson's cabins filled up right now."

Simon said: "I'm a newspaperman, and Mr. Morrell doesn't like newspapermen, so things become awkward for me."

"Is that so?" the youth said, his voice rising. "Well, sir, you'll be right welcome at our place. We ain't got much but you're welcome. Ain't that so, Eve?"

"You betcher," the girl said.

"We live further up in the hills, camping with a big trailer," the youth said. "Prospecting, kind of. I'm Marty Kraus, and this is my wife, Eve Kraus. You bet." They both laughed from sheer zest for life, as the truck drew near the cabin.

"And my name's Simon Coll," said Simon with an answering laugh.

"I'm right glad to know you, Mr. Coll."

"Mr. Coll, are you from England?" Eve asked suddenly.

"Yes, I'm from south-west England."

"You may find it hard to believe, but you're the very first Englishman I ever set eyes on," Eve said, and her eyes were rounded as a child's. "I'll be very glad if you can come and visit with us."

"I'd like that very much," Simon said.

The truck pulled up in a cloud of dust. Laughing Water's cabin stood a hundred yards back and much higher than the road. No one appeared there, the door was closed, there was no sign of movement.

"Sure you'll be okay?" Eve Kraus asked.

"I'll be quite all right," said Simon. "Thanks very much." He waved as they started off, stood watching the truck, until it was out of sight. He wished that the door of the cabin would open, that there would be some sign of life. The familiar feeling of unrest, half-excitement, half-fear, swept over him.

He reached the cabin itself.

There could be no more than three rooms. The door was in the middle, and there was a window at either side. Two wooden benches, bleached by the sun, stood under the shade of the verandah roof. The strangest thing was the silence. Simon had never known silence like it.

He went up two steps to the verandah. After a pause, he stepped to the door and banged on it with his fist; there was no response. He tried the latch, but the door was barred from the inside. The windows had outside shutters, in place, and tightly closed. He banged again, and then stepped back. He was acutely disappointed but reminded himself that there was a back as well as a front to a house. He walked round to it. Here, he was in shadow, in most welcome coolness. He could see by the quality of the light that it could not be long before sunset. He found the back door. A water-barrel, and a hanging canvas drip-bag for keeping water cool were near. The cabin was built very close to the red rock behind it; there was no way up there, for the cliff towered at least four hundred feet above him.

Then he heard a sound.

His heart began to thump, and he stared towards the back door. Wood creaked. He clenched his teeth tightly as he watched, reminding himself that Morrell or Morrell's men might take a risk—and Morrell was always likely to act on impulse.

There was a movement at a screened window, he couldn't be

81

sure what it was. Then followed the sound of a bar being drawn back, and the back door opened a few inches.

"Simon," Judith Raynor said very quietly, "are you alone?"

The whisper was so low-pitched, so redolent of fear, that it made him feel as if great danger loomed as they stood there. He moistened his lips, and said: "Yes."

Judith opened the door wider and now he could see her whole figure. "I heard the truck but I couldn't see if you were alone," she said. "Come right in, Simon. I don't want anyone to know that I'm here."

She stood back, and opened the door wider.

He was voiceless with astonishment, for he had been quite sure that Judith would stay in New York. As the sense of shock began to fade, he felt a sharp surge of annoyance; they had struck a bargain, and there was no sense in her breaking it. Didn't she trust him to do what he promised?

The cabin was dark, and surprisingly cool. He could make out a big fireplace, chairs, a bed in one corner, skin rugs, some gleaming brasses, rough log walls. Judith closed the door, and brought disappointment crashing down on him.

"Laughing Water's not here," she said.

"Where——" he began, and broke off.

"He sent me a telegram," Judith explained, as if the words hurt her. "To New York. He said that he wanted to see me urgently, and he was in great trouble. I flew to Williams yesterday, and drove as near as I could in a hired jeep, and walked the rest during the night. No one knows I'm here."

It was easier to see her now he was becoming accustomed to the gloom. Her eyes seemed very bright, deepened by the fear he had seen in them so often before.

"And he was gone when I arrived," Judith said.

"But if he sent for you——" Simon began, but broke off, again seeing an obvious significance, swiftly understanding her tension. "Have you any idea which way he went?"

"No," she said. "His best rifle's gone. He took his old bowie knife, too, and his ammunition belt. If I hadn't had the message I would have thought that he had gone hunting. But he wouldn't have gone without leaving a message pinned to the table. That was what he always did when he was going away." She moistened her lips. "We have to try to help him, Simon, we just have to."

Simon's mouth was dry, his eyes were stinging from the dust, but everything in the room was becoming clearer.

On one of the bare walls hung a lifebelt, and printed on it was

U.S.A. Chespeak. The word seemed to scream at him—a pale white circle against the time-darkened walls.

"If he took his rifle and the knife he might have gone deliberately," he argued. "And if he thought it was safer away from here he might go without leaving a message—in case the wrong people got that message." When Judith didn't respond, he went on: "Do you know where he would hide, if he's gone into hiding?"

"I know several possible places in the mountains."

"Places very few people would know?"

"Places which he and my father would keep to themselves or just tell me about," Judith said. "Little canyons where they've prospected. But——"

"Yes?"

"Some of them are three or four days' journey from here, on foot. And you couldn't get to them any other way, not even by mule. Simon, you——"

"My legs will carry me wherever I want them to go," he said gruffly. "And I'm getting used to the heat." For the first time he realised that he was still carrying the hold-all, and he slipped it off his shoulders. "What do you want to do, Judy? Start out as soon as it's dark?"

"We can't go far without light, the trail's too rocky and treacherous," Judith said. "We could walk for an hour or two, and start again as soon as dawn breaks." She was moving towards an open door on the right. "I've filled four water-bottles, and rolled two blankets—it gets chilly in the mountains at night. I've made a sack of some food, too." She looked round. "Did you once tell me that you can use a gun?"

"I can use a rifle," he assured her. He saw two rifles in a tall case by the side of the fireplace, and tried to open the doors. They were locked.

"The key is between the two big stones in the hearth," Judith called. There was more firmness in her voice, confidence which he had given to her—perhaps relief that he had been so ready to start out. "The ammunition is in a box at the bottom of the case, and there is a spare belt hanging up."

Simon found the key, opened the case, and took out a rifle. Its balance was perfect, and he could smell the faint odour of oil. He took out both guns, slipped the belt off a big brass-headed nail, and fastened it round his waist. He had to tighten it by two notches beyond its usual one. Judith came back briskly, carrying two rolls of blankets and a small sack.

"We have enough water and food for four days," she said,

83

"and I know of several places where my father and Laughing Water kept stores of both food and water." She went to a bench, picked up a belt and slung it round her waist, and he saw the handle of a revolver. "I won't take a rifle," she said. "It will get in my way." She hesitated. "Simon," she went on slowly, "you know the risk we're taking, don't you?"

"I know the risk," he said gruffly. "Don't start thinking that any of this is your fault." Quite suddenly, he put his arms out to her, and she gripped his hands. "I would rather be here than any place in the world," he said, and as the impulsive words came out he realised that he meant it. The thought had not been in his mind a moment before, yet once there, it remained as steadfast as a rock.

"I know," Judith said. "I know."

He could see every feature of her face, could see the way her lips parted, could see them trembling. He did not know what would have followed but for the sound of approaching footsteps.

Chapter 14

WARNING

Simon felt the sudden tension in the pressure of Judith's fingers, then she freed herself, turned, and tip-toed across the room towards the kitchen. The footsteps came again, creaking now on the boards outside the front door. There was something furtive about them, as there was about the guarded tap at the door. Simon slipped out the back way, the dust helping to muffle his footsteps. The sun was shining only on the top of the great cliff above him, filling this cliff side with a strange, crimson light. He reached the corner of the house, and peered along towards the front door.

Andy Lapp was straightening up from the door. He was alone. His right hand was at his bulging shirt, and against the strange light he looked more gnome than human being.

"Looking for me?" Simon asked.

The old man spun round.

"Land sakes!" he gasped. "You skeered the breath out of me!" Now he faced Simon, breathing hard. "Yes, sir, I'm looking for you. You betcher."

"Why?"

"Listen, Mister," Andy Lapp said. "I don't want any part in murder. I just want to tell you that Ma Neilson, she made a telephone call to some guy at Big Bend. Name of Gatz. And Gatz came in soon after you had left, with two other guys. They didn't know I was around, and I heard Gatz say he was laying to fix you tonight. Them's his very words, Mister—he was aiming to fix you tonight. Ma said to be careful, she told him all about the talk you had with the newspaper folk in New York, but the galoot said never mind that, he said he could fix it so it would look like an accident. I had to take some oil up to they young couple camping in the hills, and they told me where you was. I parked in Maple Canyon, I didn't want no one from Red Rock to see where I come. I don't ask nothing for the tip-off, Mister, I'm just warning you. But I'm asking you not to tell a soul it was me."

"I won't tell a soul," Simon promised. "Andy, I won't ever be able to thank you enough."

"I don't hold with murder," said Andy Lapp. "If you ask me, this goes a heck of a long way to prove that Tom Raynor, he was murdered. You betcher. I wouldn't trust no one, not even Lew Morrell himself. If I was you I would do what Ma Neilson advised. I would get on board that Western Flyer to Albuquerque. You still got time."

He peered up into Simon's face, and then suddenly shook his own head, vigorously.

"So you won't go. Okay, okay, I always did admire a guy with guts, Mister, but me, I'd prefer to be a live coward than a dead hero. I brought some packs of emergency rations. I thought maybe you would find them useful." He drew out a bulging packet from his shirt, in a small canvas bag with a tie-string at the neck. "There's just one place you can hide, and that's in Red Mountains. Don't you stay here tonight, Mister."

"I won't stay here," Simon promised.

The little man thrust the bag forward, and as Simon took it, slipped away with crab-like speed across the rocky ground towards the place where he had hidden his car.

Quickly, urgently, Simon turned back to Judith who had brought the packs she had prepared to the open door. He slung his round his shoulders, and closed the door. Now there was a faint afterglow, but none of the brightness of the sun as they moved away. The lights of a car, heading along the road, grew stronger.

Silently Judith led the way to some rock outcrops, savage of contour, seemingly impregnable. Sure-footed she led him step by step until she judged they were well enough hidden.

"We can wait here," she said. "They'll never see us."

She was breathing hard but her early training had been as ruthless as his, and both had weathered the climb without exhaustion. Simon watched the car, and longed to aim a bullet at the windscreen. He kept his rifle slung, and shifted the position of the sack which Andy Lapp had given him. The car was long and sleek, and they could see the red tinge which the rear lights spread over the cloud of dust behind it. It slowed down, and then stopped. Two men got out, and went to the back, threw up the trunk lid, and lifted out something heavy. They moved towards the cabin with careful precision. There was no sound of their footsteps, the dust made sure of that. It was impossible to see what they were carrying.

Judith said sharply: "It's a kerosene stove."

"A stove?"

"Yes," she said. "Oh God, what makes men behave like that?"

"Like what?"

"Two or three times each year one of those kerosene stoves catches fire and burns down a cabin," she said. "They're very dangerous, but they're cheap and easy to light. Poor whites, Indians and Mexicans use them. Laughing Water always cooked with charcoal or wood; he used oil only for lamps." She watched as the men heaved the stove to the back of the house.

"They won't start a fire unless they know I'm there," Simon said gruffly.

"They believe that you are there," she said. "They know you went in and they haven't seen you come out. Look!" She saw them move long planks of wood against the outer frames of the door and the windows at the front, to make sure that they couldn't be opened from the inside, then carry the stove to the back.

The light was failing rapidly. Little sound came, but the men watched the back door and the back window closely. They pushed the stove close to the back door, and blocked the door. They bent over the stove; it looked as if they were pouring something over it.

Simon said: "They can't be setting fire to it *now*. They haven't made sure that I'm inside."

"They think you're lying low," Judith said, "waiting for them to go away. Simon, this is how Morrell *always* works. He never waits to make sure, before taking action."

There was a sudden flare in the hands of one of the men, and a moment later a ball of fire curled in an arc towards the oil stove. The men stood back as it struck the stove, and a sheet of flame spread vivid light, shining angrily on the nearby rocks, showing up every part of the cabin and the outbuildings. The glow expanded rapidly, leaping upwards to lick at the roof; in a few seconds the roof was blazing. The two men were running towards the car, and the light seemed to chase them for a few seconds, then to give them up, while the flames caught the corners and the sides of the cabin, leaping higher and spreading wider.

The men reached the car.

Simon said savagely: "We should have killed the devils. We ought to go down now and——"

"No," Judith said sharply. "Let them think you were in it. They don't know that I'm here, and if they think you're dead we'll have a start." She was breathing agitatedly, and the light from the fire of the old man's shack shimmered on her eyes and made bronze beauty of her face. "Simon," she said. "Now we know one more positive fact."

He looked at her, his jaws clamped, hands clenched, trapped in his own fury. The car began to move away, and the flames rose higher. He knew exactly what Judith meant, and the 'positive fact' had been fermenting in his mind almost from the moment that Andy Lapp had come with the warning.

In spite of the telephone call to New York, in spite of the danger which would come if the police sent out a search party, Morrell's men meant to kill him.

"But why should it matter so much to Morrell?" demanded Judith helplessly. "What harm could you do to him?" When Simon did not answer, she went on: "They must have realised you were coming to see Laughing Water, that may be what drove him away. Simon—why do you matter to them?"

The question, in a different form, was tossing about in his own restless mind. "*Who am I?*" Once he knew the answer to that he could be able to answer Judith's question. A dozen lights were on in the town, and from it two cars set out suddenly. Judith said:

"Someone's coming to see what the fire's about."

Simon said nothing. Facts hammered themselves into his mind, and the one he hated the most was about Judith. She had not been in any danger until he had arrived. During the twelve months which had followed her father's death, during the law suit, in all the time she could have given evidence against Lewis Morrell, she had not been in physical danger. Now she was. Marchesi, dead;

87

Laughing Water Smith driven away perhaps to his death; Judith, in as great danger as he.

Why was it happening?

He wanted to urge her to face the truth; that by herself she would be safe, that there was nothing to prevent her from catching the Western Flyer back to civilisation. But he could see that she had already faced it, and made her decision. Nothing he said now would alter it.

"Is it too late to start tonight?" he asked gruffly.

"There's a trail we can walk for the next two hours," she answered. "The stars will give us some light." She led the way past the place where the Krauses were camping.

The thick dust of the trail muffled their footsteps as they walked on, the glow of the camp fire soon behind them. Further away, only a faint haze of light against the distant darkness, was the township of Red Rock.

* * *

Simon lay, drowsy, with the blanket over him, the bright stars above so near that it seemed almost possible to speak to them, and hear their reply. He heard Judith's soft breathing, and believed her to be asleep. They were in a recess between great rocks, shut off from the world.

He found himself wondering whether they would ever get back.

* * *

He heard a movement, and immediately edged himself up to a sitting position. Judith's blanket lay flattened and flung aside, but there was no sign of her. Suddenly she appeared from the other side of a rock. Her hair was rumpled, and her face still flushed from sleep. She looked wholly feminine, young, lovely. She stopped at sight of him, raising a hand casually.

"Hi."

"How long have you been awake?"

"Five minutes, I guess," Judith said. "You want to know what I want most?"

"Breakfast?"

"A bath," she said. "The most desirable and least attainable luxury I can think of at the moment. Will you get some more sticks, so we can get hot coffee?"

"Where are we heading?"

"Towards a waterfall," she answered. "There are three on this side of the mountains, which run into the Colorado, and they won't be in flood right now. There's one thing civilisation does for you—it gives you instant coffee. Would you rather have a good hot meal now, or cold later?"

"Shouldn't we get moving while it's cool?"

"One day I'll take you hunting," she said. There was gaiety in her voice, as if the solitude and vastness of the hills had driven fear away. "I think you would like that."

Half-an-hour afterwards they were packed up again, and on the trail. They walked steadily between rocks, flints and small stones underfoot. Now they were on the higher slopes of the foothills. The silence about them was still the most impressive thing to Simon; the silence and the vastness. Judith walked as if she had forgotten he was with her. When she stopped he saw the sadness was back in her eyes; tension was in her, too.

"We can take a side trip along here," she said, "and then we can see over the desert." She waited for Simon, then led the way through a narrow gap in the rocks. She knew the folds of the land, the fissures, the trails and the hidden places as well as Simon knew the folds of the Dorset hills. She climbed up nimbly, hardly aware of her pack, then crouching low, looked down into the desert. She put her hand to her belt and took out a small pair of field glasses. As she stood with them at her eyes, her slim body upright, poised, provocative, he saw it stiffen. She put the glasses down abruptly.

"Come and look at this."

Simon scrambled up to her side. At first he could see only the arid waste of desert.

"Nearer," she said. "In the foothills." She put a hand up and guided the glasses. "Focus on that big hill to the west, and then follow it down. Near Laughing Water Smith's cabin."

Simon felt the coolness of her fingers, and their hard pressure; then he saw the hill, which seemed to leap towards him. He kept it in his line of vision until it shone upon a man walking. He saw others; a dozen or more, all moving towards the camp where the young couple were—all on this trail.

"Search party," he said, drily.

"Search party is right," Judith echoed, and after a long pause, she said: "They aren't going to let you get away."

"Could they be a hunting party?"

"Simon, they know now that you weren't in the cabin, and they're coming after you," she said. "Don't fool yourself. They're

Morrell's men, they're all carrying rifles."

Simon put the glasses to his eyes again, and watched the men. They were drawing steadily nearer, and he began to wonder how much start he and Judith had, and whether it was enough.

"There will be another party, with a jeep," she said. "They'll go a long way round, and both lots will try to hem us in. If we hurry, we might get ahead of both.".

"Judith," Simon said.

"We can talk as we go," she declared. She jumped down and began to stride towards the main trail.

He caught up with her. "Judy, where can we stand and fight them?"

"*Fight?*" she echoed. "There are twenty at least."

"I know," he said, "but I'm tired of running away. I haven't been running for long, but I'm sick of it already. If we run, they'll get nearer and nearer——" He saw the astonishment growing in her eyes, and went on stubbornly: "If we fight back, they won't do any more harm than if they simply catch us running."

They were striding up the trail, where there was less dust but many more stones. In places they had to jump over small cracks in the earth.

"Five miles up there's a place called Little Neck," she said. "Beyond it there's only one trail to take, on foot, or horseback or by mule. If we can get beyond Little Neck, they'll have to follow on behind, they won't be able to encircle us. If they get there first——" She broke off, and after a moment added savagely: "I know what I'm talking about. At Little Neck only seventy years ago, a hundred settlers and prospectors were cut off by the Nhovi and the Sioux, who had a raiding party here. There were only a dozen survivors, one of them my own grandfather. If we don't get past Little Neck camp, we won't have any chance to fight or to run. And it's five miles, five steep miles away."

Chapter 15

LITTLE NECK CAMP

Now the sun really burned, and there was no shelter from it. Rocks which towered high at the side of the trail were jet black with shadow, but where Judith and Simon had to walk, the burning rays shone straight down on them, and with every minute seemed to get hotter. The long, easy strides of the first half hour had become shorter, more deliberate, effortful steps. The trail, which had been slightly uphill, became steep and precipitous. Every step had to be taken with great care. Now and again, Simon dislodged a stone and heard it falling over a ridge of rock, down on to the trail, gathering other stones with it so that there was a rattle which lasted for fully a minute.

On either side were the sheer walls of the red canyon. It was like Red Gorge, but much narrower, so that in places there was only just room to pass; and there would be no room at all for horse or mule. The sides were broken and sharp and angry. The dust underfoot was sometimes ankle deep, so that they ploughed through it heavily, every step a drag on their muscles. Judith was staring at the trail ahead, eyes narrowed and lips set tightly, as if this pressure was too much for her. Simon kept ten yards behind; she might slip and fall—as he might, also. Now and again they rested, as if by mutual consent, and sat for a few minutes on a rock, to look downward watchfully. Whenever he did this, it seemed to Simon impossible to realise that they had climbed so far already. It was like looking into a great ravine, while further down the rock-strewn path seemed impassable.

Now and again they paused, to listen; and they heard the falling stones, occasionally the cry of a bird.

Simon did not know how far they had come, and did not ask; words took breath, and every ounce was needed. They stopped together to rest, and started off again after a nod from one or from the other. Each time they stopped, Simon saw lizards on the sun-drenched rocks, saw them start as sound and shadow approached, saw them vanish. There was no other living things. There was just the heat and the dryness, parching their mouths, getting into their eyes. The sun struck the savage rock and bounced back at them, searing all exposed flesh.

Judith turned towards a flat boulder, which stood in the shadow at the side of the trail, as if at last she had to stop for shade as well as rest. Simon unscrewed the cap of the water bottle, and handed it to her.

"How far?"

"Quite close now. Listen."

It was like straining the ears for silence itself. Except for their breathing and the occasional scream of a bird, there was no sound. Then Simon heard a throbbing note. It seemed a long way off, but it was quite unmistakable. He saw the alarm that sprang to her eyes.

"That's a jeep," she said.

"Is it—near?"

"It's on the far side of Little Neck," she said, with absolute conviction. "It's as near Little Neck as we are, but has to go a long way round."

"How far are we away?"

"Half-an-hour," Judith answered tensely. "There's one short cut, but——" She hesitated. "I should have brought rope. I didn't think they would set out so soon. If we take a chance——"

"Can we get there before them, if we take that chance?"

"We might."

"Let's go," he said. "Let's see what kind of a chance it is." He guessed what she meant, for they could see the top of the canyon, the jagged rock where climbing would be deadly dangerous, and where a rope might be the only way to save one's life.

As they walked on, step after painful step, he kept thinking of the jeep. There was an almost overwhelming temptation to pause and listen again, but that would be throwing away precious seconds. The trail narrowed until it was little more than a defile, then vanished in a sharp curve. Just in front of the curve were a dozen natural steps in the rock.

Judith stopped.

"That's the short cut," she said, jerkily. "We can get up there in ten minutes—if we're lucky. The other way will take us half-an-hour."

She stopped and raised her head. The throbbing note of the jeep was still clearly audible. A tiny reddish brown chipmunk darted across their path. A bird hovered high above them: eagle or buzzard, Simon was not sure which.

If they had a rope, the climb would be hard but not really difficult, but if they started up and were unable to get further, they would be trapped. Three buzzards were now hovering overhead, and as Simon looked up into the startling blue of the sky, he saw two more, flying in wider circles further away.

"I'll go first," he said.

Judith made no comment. Simon moved off the trail and clambered over the nearer rocks. He did not glance down, but tested every foothold and every handhold with his full weight, to make sure that he did not loosen any stone which would fall on Judith. He reached a ledge, and stood close to the sheer face of the cliff. To the right and left were broken rocks which could be climbed, but he could not reach them, for the ledge petered out. He could just see the top of the cliff, and judged that it was fifty feet above. It reminded him of the way the Coll had been sliced away, leaving a sheer drop into the sea.

There were holes in the face of the rock. He could see the scratches where men with steel-capped boots had climbed before. He studied that bare face closely, then stretched up for a hand-hold, half an arm's length away. He hauled himself up, body pressed against the rock, sharp edges biting into his knees. He found foothold. He stood on one foot, face close to the rock now, unable to look downwards, hardly able to turn his head. He peered up, saw a shadowy mark within arm's reach, and stretched towards it; yes, it was a hole large enough for him to use.

He took what weight he could on his fingers, and hauled himself up again, but desperately needed some other purchase for foot or hand. The strain on his fingers was excruciating. Sharp pains began to shoot through them, through the back of his hand, and along his wrist. He was beginning to gasp for breath. If he couldn't get a firmer hold, he would have to let go; he hadn't a chance of holding on, he would have to let go——

His left hand touched the edge of another small cavity. He gripped the bottom of it, and hauled himself up. Sweat was dripping off him, and he was breathing through his open mouth. He couldn't be sure how far below Judith was.

He could not hear the jeep now, only the drumming of blood in his own ears, and the screeching of birds. A shadow fell upon the rock just in front of his face; he felt like screaming at the buzzard which cast the shadow, and he clenched his teeth until his jaws threatened to crack. He slid one hand over the hot surface of the rock, as far as it would go, and then found a thick ledge, something thick enough to grip. He saw that it was the cliff top he had noticed from below, but it was further to his right than he had hoped. He leaned towards it, groping for, and finding, another outcrop with his foot. Cautiously he edged along, until his face was on a level with the ledge. The wild sense of triumph made his heart thump more violently; because this ledge was wide enough to stand on. He got both hands to it, called: "*We're there!*" and made a final haul, got a foot on to the ledge, and his leg over. In a moment he was crouching safely, still gasping, eyes filled with tears of pain from the little clouds of dust.

Slowly, he turned round.

Judith was still some distance down the rock face, and as he studied her position he saw that she could not come the way he had come because she was not quite tall enough. She was spread-eagled against the rock, her face upturned towards him—and he doubted if she could get a yard further by herself.

His heart gave an agonising lurch of pain. He eased himself back from the rim of the ledge, and shrugged his roll off his back. He unrolled the blanket, nicked it with his knife and ripped it down; he could not move fast enough to ease his wild anxiety. He tied the two strips together, knotted each end so that they would not unfurl, then leaned over the cliff as far as he could go.

"Try and hold this!"

She was looking to the right, now; she had made a foot or more of progress in that direction, but was stuck again. It seemed a long time before she turned her head towards him, shadowed by the dark shape of a buzzard, hovering between her and the top of the ledge. Simon heard the rustle of its passing. A buzzard was probably safe enough, but an eagle might attack. My God, an eagle might attack! He glanced up, desperately. He could no longer see the bird. He felt a new kind of fear which drove him almost to panic.

"*Take hold of this!*" he called again.

Now Judith was looking upwards, chin almost touching the rock. The blanket dangled a foot or two above her head. With agonising slowness, she moved her right arm towards it. She was immediately underneath the blanket, now, but could not touch it. He edged further forward to dangle it lower. If he went too far he would risk falling over, and if either of them fell, they would crash to death. The lower knot of the blanket looked as if it were within her grasp. He saw her fingers, curling about it. He saw the way she strained her body so as to clutch the blanket above the knot—and he saw her clench her hand.

"*I'll pull!*" he called. "Just hold on!"

"*Pull*," she called back. "I'm ready."

He took the blanket in both hands, and leaned his whole weight against it. For the first few seconds he was able to see down the face of the cliff, but soon he drew too far back. Back, back, back he leaned, with that dead weight dragging on him, and the blanket scraping perilously against the sharp edge of the ledge. He felt as if he were losing consciousness, as the sun beat merciless fire on his head. He could not take the strain much longer; *he could not take the strain.*

Then, quite suddenly, the pressure eased.

For a moment, he could think only of physical relief, then realised what might have happened. Judith might have let go,

94

might have fallen. He inched towards the ledge again, almost afraid to look down, but saw her hands in a hole only a foot beneath him. The rest would be easy.

Easy.

*   *   *

There was a long gash in Judith's jeans. There was an ugly scratch on her forehead, above the right eye. Her fingers were grazed. There was blood on her chin. She lay on her back, eyes closed, gulping in great shuddering breaths—she had spent herself to the limit, and could not go on. Yet the throbbing of that jeep was forever in Simon's ears, and the slowly weaving shadows of the giant birds were never far away. He stood up to his full height. Yes, it was easy now, a steep climb but on fairly even ground. He unscrewed the cap of his water bottle.

She didn't open her eyes, but moved her lips, which were thickly caked with red dust as he moistened them.

She moved her lips again.

"You go on," she said, hoarsely. "Go on."

He screwed the cap back, and pushed the life-saving blanket to one side.

"Sit up," he ordered sharply. And then again: "Sit up!" She began to move her body, but not easily, and he wondered if she was hurt as well as exhausted. "Sit straight up." He helped her, until she was sitting upright. "Now listen," he said. "When I lift you, relax completely. Understand?"

She opened her eyes.

"Simon, you go on," she begged. "You go on."

"I'm going on all right," he said, "but how long do you think I'd last out here without you?" He put one arm round her waist, and slid the other beneath her knees. Staggering upright, he steadied himself, and began to walk forward. The 'easy' climb was steeper than he expected, but he could make it step by step, and there were some level stretches. He kept going, legs moving automatically. The sun was like a licking fire, the heat so great that the air seemed to burn. It seared his back, his legs, his head, his neck. He held Judith against his breast; and as he staggered forward there were moments when he almost forgot the reason and the purpose of this journey.

He felt Judith stir.

"All right," he muttered. "We're all right."

"Let me down," she said. Words were an effort for both of

them, almost as great a physical effort as movement. She paused between each word. "Let me down," she pleaded. "I can walk."

He lowered her slowly to her feet. She staggered, held tightly to his arm, then began to walk. There was a drumming sound in his ears but he did not know whether it was the jeep or his own blood pounding. The shadows of the hideous birds had gone. They walked on for two or three minutes, then came to a clearing. Nestling against high rocks were a dozen wooden cabins. Close to these were two bare skeletal trees. There were water barrel, tie-rails, benches, places for camp fires. There was a tall flagpole, with the *Stars and Stripes* hanging limply from it. There was that throbbing sound. It was coming from a trail to the right, perhaps two hundred yards away—the only trail which opened out into this clearing and large enough for a jeep. He could not tell how far away it was.

"How far——" he asked hoarsely.

She didn't answer.

"Judy," he said, urgently. "Can we get away from them?"

She said: "No." She closed her eyes, and went on: "No, they're too near, we can't get away."

The sense of failure and despair robbed her voice of all emotion and all feeling.

Chapter 16

THE JEEP

Judith's words were echoing in Simon's mind as he went forward towards the place where the trail debouched into the clearing. She called out something, but he could not catch the words. He tried to hurry, but his legs were still stiff, the muscles painfully knotted. He slid the rifle off his shoulder. He thought he heard Judith call out again, but could not be sure.

The sound of the jeep's engine was much louder now than it had been; any moment he thought that it might swing into sight. But when he reached the opening, and the rocks which guarded it, it was still out of sight. The trail here, narrowed to a track between the sheer sides of rock walls. Could that be blocked? He moistened his lips, and tasted the dust bitter and hard on his tongue. He looked about him, but saw no rocks large enough to

96

roll towards the trail and stop the jeep—if there were three or four men to help roll and push then it could be done, but he and Judith could not hope to, even had they been fresh and full of vigour.

He looked round at Judith.

She was coming forward slowly, taking short, unsteady steps, and he thought she was calling urgently. The rumbling now became a roar, so the jeep could not be far away. He thought of running, of making Judith run, too, but it would be useless; the car would be able to outpace them easily. The trail sloped downwards sharply to a tall rock, spiked like a bayonet, and as he reached it he caught his first glimpse of the jeep.

There were four men in it. He did not recognise three of the four, but could not mistake the tall figure or the hard face of the man Gatz.

They carried rifles. One man, beside the driver, had his rifle cocked. The others were sitting back at ease. The trail itself was very narrow. On a straight road they were only half-a-minute away; on a trail like this, perhaps five minutes. Simon studied the position, coldly dispassionate. They had no room to turn round. Whatever happened, they would have to come on, or stay where they were. They had no cover except the jeep itself; no rocks on the trail were big enough to hide them.

There was a small sound behind him.

He said: "I'm going to pick them off, one by one."

"Simon," Judith said.

"It's no use trying to stop the jeep, they can walk from there," Simon said. "There are only four of them." He levelled the gun. He heard Judith's laboured breathing. He did not glance round at her. He knew that the world would say that he ought to call a warning, but he knew what warning these men would give him, if they once reached him.

"Simon," Judith said, "let them get—get nearer. Then I can use the revolver."

"How near?"

"Another—ten yards."

He looked round, and saw that she held the gun in her right hand. She was just behind him, and from where they stood, they could see down the trail without being seen.

The jeep groaned upwards, turning right and left to avoid boulders; obviously none of the men had the slightest suspicion of impending trouble. They drew nearer. Simon kept the rifle levelled, his eyes narrowed against the glare of the sun.

"Nearer?" he asked.

"Yes."

"I'll take Gatz, who's driving, and the man next to him," Simon said. "You wait until the others jump down."

He waited for another half second, then got the driver in his sights, and fired. The sharp recoil of the shot put him momentarily off his balance, but he was ready again before the men on the jeep realised what had come upon them. Gatz dropped his hands from the steering wheel. The man next to him half rose from his seat. Simon fired again.

The other two men were now on their feet, alarm stark on their faces. He heard the sharp retort of Judith's gun; the men were so near that it was almost impossible to miss. He got another in his sights, and fired, while the jeep began to sag backwards down the steep slope, out of control. One man toppled forward, falling to the ground. Gatz was pinned between the steering wheel and the back of his seat. All four men were wounded, and out of the hunt, while one of them might well be dead.

Simon said: "Let's go." He put an arm round Judith, as she slid the revolver back into its holster. A man was screaming curses at them, and the shrill venom of his voice came out of the narrow trail and spread wide about the clearing. They were walking with longer strides as hope and confidence came back. To Simon, the incredible thing was that the urgent danger had gone, and that they could now dare to relax. They might have won a day's reprieve, or two, or even three.

As they neared the first of the cabins, he saw a notice, of large black lettering burnt into wood:

Emergency Supplies and Water.
Key in Case.

There was a small glass covered case fastened to the wall and the key was inside it.

"How much time in hand have we got now?"

"Four or five hours," Judith answered.

"How far on can we be then?"

She turned to look at him. The blood had caked on her forehead and chin; he saw blood on her cheek, too, and for the first time wondered what he himself looked like. Her eyes were grave, much as they had been when he had first seen her in Wegel's office. Wegel's office, nearly three thousand miles away—a civilisation away.

"We can be in the heart of the hills, and they will only find us by luck," she answered. "We can always keep away from them, but——" She broke off.

"But?"

"There are only three ways out of the mountains," she said slowly. "They could guard each trail—the one we've come from, the one where the jeep came from, the one near Big Bend. We can't hope to cross the mountains to the east or the north; they're impassable except to a big expedition."

"It can only be a matter of time," Simon urged. "It won't be long before the *Unity Agency* or the police——"

She stopped him with a gesture.

"You can't rely on them," she said. "You can't rely on anybody, here. Remember how much more Morrell's men will hate us after this. Even if Morrell himself told them to stop, they would almost certainly try to kill us."

A curious confidence rose in Simon, because they had been so near death yet were alive.

"We've at least four hours, you say? How long do we need to get ourselves lost?"

"Three hours," Judith answered.

"If there's water here, then we ought to have a good wash," Simon said. "And some coffee. Have we time for that cooked meal?"

"Just coffee," she said. "There's a shower here—and an oil stove. An oil stove——"

Did a picture of last night's fire appear in her mind, too?

*　　*　　*

Simon heard the water splashing as Judith took a shower, where he had not dreamed one would be. It was outside, a big bucket rigged up with a pulley, which emptied its contents over a sheet of metal peppered with holes. He had seen something like it, years ago, in the musical play of *South Pacific*. He had flung off his shirt, brushed down his clothes, put water for the coffee on to boil. Judith's clothes were hanging over the partition which divided the hut itself from the shower.

"Judy?"

"Hi, there!" she called.

"I'm going to beat the dust out of your clothes."

"It's a waste of time," she called, "but go ahead."

He pulled the clothes off the partition, and hung them over a rope line, used for washing. As he shook them dust rose round him in pink clouds. He looked through the cloud towards the distant peaks. He did not really see them, he saw Judith. He did not know what would happen to them now, but for a few days they would be together, and for those few days he would give thanks, humbly and fervently.

The water had stopped splashing. He took the shirt and jeans and tossed them over the partition.

"Here they come; watch out!"

"Simon, I'm going to need a needle and thread."

"Didn't you pack any?"

He heard her laugh.

"There'll be some in the shed, in a cupboard. Everything is kept here for emergency. How's that coffee?"

"Coming up!"

She laughed again.

"I'll go and get that needle and thread," he called. He went into the hut, found the cupboard, and the box he was looking for. Through the partially open door he glimpsed Judith. Her hair was damp, and curled close to her head, outlining its boyish shape and her broad forehead. Her look of childlike innocence, her vulnerability as she stood there unconscious of his glance, touched his heart with such a rush of tenderness that he stayed fiddling with the box longer than necessary. When at last he turned, she was smiling at him.

"Your turn for a shower," she called lightly. "Si, you really look a wreck. I'm beginning to wonder what I looked like when we came here."

He said simply: "You looked wonderful."

Her smile began to fade, but it did not die altogether. She stood very still. He was reminded of that moment in Laughing Water's cabin—and he knew what could so easily happen, now, and knew that it must not, yet.

He forced his expression to one becoming to a brotherly fellow-traveller, as he repeated heartily:

"And you still look wonderful! Don't drink all of that coffee." He pushed past her, filled a bucket from one of the barrels, and made for the shower.

When he rejoined her, two or three minutes later, she was sitting cross-legged on a stone seat, facing one of the open fireplaces, and the unbelievable panorama of the mountains. The coffee was steaming in an enamel mug. There were sandwiches, too.

He felt as if they were alone in the world.

When they left, there was another blanket rolled round for him to carry, replacing the torn one, and they had repacked the food and emergency supplies, so that each carried a small sack. They had said little during the meal, and said very little now. Ahead was a wide canyon, and for as far as Simon could see the walking would be fairly straightforward. Except for the sound of their footsteps, the silence seemed absolute, a deadening barrier cutting them off from the rest of the world. Simon had never known such stillness. A sense of infinity seemed to lie upon him, so that he felt quiet in mind, and strangely humble.

He did not think of the men whom he had shot, but only of the past hour. And he thought of how much he wanted to be with Judith, in body and in spirit, to love and to cherish.

Walking with her, side by side, he slowly became conscious of some outside influence. Disturbed and alarmed he did not speak of it at first, glanced at Judith, saw her looking straight ahead as if she had seen and heard nothing. A hundred paces on, and the droning of an engine became much louder. Now she could not fail to hear it. Simon knew it to be too even for a land machine. This came from the air. The peace of mind vanished; in its place was driving anxiety.

"Judy, do you hear that?"

"It's an aeroplane," she said quietly. "I'm trying to make up my mind what kind it is."

"What kind?"

"There are some air routes across the Red Mountains," she explained. "Denver to San Francisco, and Reno to Salt Lake City. It could be a regular flight." She didn't give him any indication whether she believed that to be the case or not. The drone grew louder. It was soon so insistent that he felt sure that it must be close to the tops of the mountains—and an aircraft in regular flight would not come so low.

The engine's reverberation seemed to make even the earth tremble.

"Let's move over there," Simon said, gruffly. He took her arm, and they walked towards the cover of overhanging rocks.

Suddenly a dark shadow crossed the canyon; then he saw the silhouette of the whole aeroplane sweeping along the canyon. They reached a spot where they could crouch out of sight, but Simon saw only the black shadow. The machine was flying very slowly, as it would if its pilot were searching for something—or for someone.

"Can it land?" Simon asked, tensely.

"Only a helicopter could land here."

"Does Morrell own a helicopter?"

"He could hire one."

The dark shadow drew nearer; the noise was now so great that they covered their ears. As the sound began to fade, they watched the disappearing shadow. It was still flying low, and there was no doubt that the pilot was searching for them.

"If it turns back," Judith said, "it means that the pilot saw us."

Chapter 17

THE HIDING PLACE

The droning of the aircraft gradually faded, and the silence fell again, as if infinity had stretched out for them. They had moved from the cover of the rock and were going along the floor of the canyon. They were walking easily, but some way ahead the canyon seemed to peter out, and the hills and rocks awaited them.

They did not slacken pace until they reached the end of the canyon. Beyond them were the high mountains, with great defiles between them, a wild rugged country of such grandeur that even the bleaching sun could not rob it of its brilliance.

"Once we're there," she said, "we're absolutely safe."

"*While* we're there," he amended.

She nodded, her face sombre.

"How near are we to Laughing Water's hiding places?"

"We should reach the first one before dark," she said.

They began to climb off the level ground. Clambering over the rocks they found a patch of deep shadow for their first resting place. They sat back, with deep sighs of relief, stretching out their legs. Simon handed Judith the water bottle.

"Si," she said, "what's at the bottom of all this?"

"Good question," he said.

"Don't make light of it. Haven't you any idea at all?"

"Just what I've told you," he assured her.

"This man Marchesi was frightened of you because of who you are, and sent the radio-telegram to Morrell. So Morrell had him killed, as he had your aunt killed—and now he can't stop until you're dead."

"That's what it looks like," Simon agreed. He didn't want to talk about it now, for Morrell and Marchesi and all the mystery

102

of his past seemed so far away—and Judith was within hand's reach.

"But why?" she insisted.

"I've been trying to guess," Simon told her, "but I don't think any guess will help. We'll find the answer soon enough."

"You sound as if you know it already."

He said slowly: "All I really know is the possibility that we won't get out of here alive. And if we don't——" He shrugged his shoulders.

"And if we do?"

"Judy," Simon said, "if we do get out alive, will you marry me?"

He did not raise his voice. He did not move his body. He watched her as he spoke, so intently that he did not miss a single movement of her face, nor an instant's change of expression. He watched every feature, and he found his heart thumping with a pounding, frightening vigour. If he moved, he would go to her, if he moved it would be the breakdown in his self-restraint.

She said: "I don't know." Her voice was husky and low-pitched. "I simply don't know what I'm going to feel like when this is over. One part of my mind doesn't believe that I'll die, the other part knows that we haven't any hope of escaping alive. I don't want to think beyond—beyond this moment. Being here, being with you, finding the answers to the things we don't know. I don't want to make any decision—I tell you I don't want to think, Si. So don't make me."

"I won't make you," he promised.

*　　*　　*

Not far ahead was a mushroom-shaped rock, smoothed by the wind and the rain and the snows of centuries, and approached by a man-made gulley. Beyond was a sharp descent, and at the foot of this a ridge of rocks carved to fabulous and fantastic shapes, like turrets of a castle long since given up to nature. The evening sun was falling directly upon these, and on to the mouth of a cave.

"We'll be at the first hiding place in ten minutes," Judith said. "It's tricky ground. I'll go on by myself, you follow ten yards behind."

Suddenly she gave a gasping cry.

"There's his hat, he's here! Laughing Water!" she cried wildly. "Laughing Water!"

Simon watched her running, leaping to the bottom of the ridge.

She moved so beautifully. He was smiling, enjoying the sight of her lithe body, and the fact that she was suddenly excited and happy.

Then he saw a thin wire stretched right across the mouth of the cave. The sun caught it, turning it to silver, and he sensed what it was in a moment of horror.

"Don't go in!" he shouted desperately. *"Stop, Judy! Don't go in!"*

She missed a step, put out a hand to save herself from falling, and staggered. She was only a yard or two away from the wire. He did not know for certain what it would do if she tripped over it, but he believed he knew—believed that it would set off an explosion, that this was a booby trap mine which had been planted to blow them both to pieces.

She reeled away from the wire.

"Keep still!" he called, and she turned just her head and the upper part of her body. "There's a wire, right in front of you," he called. "Be careful, don't touch it."

He walked towards her with care and deliberation, fearful as he drew nearer that he should trip and fall. Nothing else moved until Judith, as careful as he, stepped over the wire. She followed it into the mouth of the cave, Simon following behind her. It led to a small box, which was standing flat against the side of the cave—and inside the box were sticks of dynamite, like red cardboard candles, bound together. Awed, white-faced at their escape, they realised that the cave would have been demolished and they would have been blown to their death had the sun not glinted on the wire.

In a hushed voice, Judith said: "But it's Laughing Water's hat."

* * *

Her words made the air seem cold. She picked up the battered Stetson, as Simon disconnected the fuse. She held the old hat in her hand, and stared out across this stretch of mesa land, all the colour and all the eagerness drained out of her face.

"They must have been here," she said. "They've caught him."

Simon went across to her and put his arm round her shoulders so that they stood side by side.

"Perhaps they sent men out to follow him," he said. "Some may have been here ahead of us."

They stood with their backs to the mouth of the cave which was

104

to have given them sanctuary. Nothing and no one moved. Outcrops of rock rose up in all directions, and as Simon scanned the hostile desolation, he realised how secure a hiding-place this was yet Morrell's men had found it. And if men had come here ready to set the trap, where were they now?

The sticks of dynamite were free from dust; they could not have been in the cave for long. The shimmering of the wire in the evening sunlight showed that it had been recently placed there, too—perhaps within the past hour, possibly within the past ten minutes. Now he could imagine men crouching behind every outcrop, picture them peering this way, watching, guns already cocked to shoot. He felt the stifling fear which had been with him so long, and his grip on Judith's shoulders tightened. He could feel how rigidly she was standing, as if all her nerves and muscles were as taut as the stretched wire.

Yet nothing moved.

Up here on this vast tableland the sun burned as deeply as in the valley; but that sun would soon drop below the high peaks, which looked dark and menacing already. When it fell, the coolness of evening would fall with it, but it would be light for an hour yet.

"Simon."

"Yes?"

"If anyone was watching, wouldn't they have shot at us by now?"

"You'd think so."

"We've been here for—a long time."

"Plenty of time to die," Simon said.

She pressed closer to him.

"I can't see how it happened. I can't believe that anyone would be able to find Laughing Water's hiding place. It—it's not been discovered in fifty years."

"If they followed him, they'd find it."

"He'd know he was being followed, and go somewhere else," she said. "No one knows these mountains as he does."

"He *must* have been followed," Simon insisted. "Or else there *is* someone who knows the mountains as well as he."

"Who?"

"One of Morrell's men."

"I can't believe it," Judith whispered, and looked down at the wire, harmless now. "Laughing Water and my father, and—perhaps a few trappers, a few rock hounds."

"Indians?"

"I—I suppose so. Nhovi Indians and white men."

"Poor men?"

"Mostly poor," she admitted.

"Men who could be bought," Simon said. "And now Morrell has *Transa*'s million dollars to spend on bribing." He pointed to a shallow gulley, only a few feet away. "If we go over there we can see everything, and get into the cave safely if anyone approaches."

She didn't move.

"Judy——"

"If anyone comes, we'll be driven into the cave and then they'll cut us off," she said. "We'll be trapped. It's better out here."

She was right, of course.

"What are you thinking?" he asked.

"Whether we ought to go on to the next——" she drew a deep breath—"sanctuary."

"How far away?"

"I suppose—three hours' journey."

"Hard going?"

"Across the mesa," she answered, and looked up to the sky, for the brightness of the sun was gradually fading from it, and the first dark shadows of the mountain peaks were being cast upon the lonely earth. The feeling of being alone with Judith, of being the last surviving people on the face of the earth, came back with greater vividness. He knew that men might be hiding, and that they might be watched, but he could not believe that anyone else had ever been here, could ever come now. The wire, the hat, the dynamite, the stores inside the cave, all made such a belief nonsense, yet the feeling of utter desolation grew and grew.

"Do you want to try?" he asked her.

She didn't answer.

"I'm game to," he said. "I don't fancy it, but I'm game. We can follow the stars."

"Yes," she said. "But—if they came and put this here, why aren't they watching?"

Simon said: "Guessing can't help. We'll almost certainly get it wrong." He did not want to guess, something deep within him warned him that the obvious thing—that the next hiding place would be occupied by Morrell's men—was probably the true one, and he wanted to shut his mind to it.

"Si," Judy said, "it might have been set for Laughing Water."

He started.

"To kill him?"

"Yes."

"What about his hat?"

She didn't speak.

"I think we ought to wait until it's dark," he said abruptly. "There'll be less risk of being seen." He paused. "Can we build a fire in the cave?"

"Yes."

"Now we'll see if you can really cook!"

He won a swift flash of a smile, but that was all; the shock of disappointment and the prolonged tension of fear had gone too deep into her. She began to move about, mechanically. He collected some pieces of wood and root, but when he got back to the cave, Judith had already kindled a fire from wood stacked near the opening. Bacon strips were in a big frying pan, and she was mixing powdered egg in an enamel bowl.

As she bent over the fire, he wondered how often she had cooked like this. She knew the mountains as well as any man, he told himself; they were an important part of her life. She had been coming here since childhood. She knew exactly where her father and Laughing Water Smith had their hiding places, their stores of food. She had come hunting and prospecting with them —she must know nearly as much as the two older men.

"Judy."

"Hm—hmm?"

"Where did your father die?"

She quickened the pace of her beating.

"Near—near the next hiding place."

"Do you know what he was coming to look for?"

"I've told you—no."

"He found something of great value, probably this gold—and they killed him to make sure that he couldn't take it himself. Is that what you think?"

"What else can I think?" she demanded.

"I've been considering the facts I know, not the guesswork," Simon said. He watched as she tipped the beaten eggs into the frying pan. "The facts," he repeated. "Your father went out on one of his usual hunting or prospecting expeditions."

"Yes."

"And didn't come back, because he was buried under a fall of rock."

"Yes."

"He sent word back, by Laughing Water Smith."

She didn't answer.

"Judy, did he send word back by Laughing Water?"

107

She closed her eyes, as if with great pain.

"Judy," he said insistently, "tell me the truth. Tell me everything you know. What happened exactly?"

"Laughing Water brought back the news of the fall, and took out a party to find the body."

"And brought your father back."

"Yes."

"Who said it was murder?"

"I did, to begin with," Judith said. "There were some newspapermen out here, and I said I didn't believe that my father would ever let himself be killed by these mountains, he knew them too well. He wouldn't walk where the rock might fall—he simply wouldn't go there. He could tell the condition of the rocks at a glance. I said that someone must have engineered that fall."

"Who did you say that to?"

She opened her eyes wide. "To one of these newspapermen. It was just after I'd sold the claim."

"The claim to the land?"

"The lease of the prospecting rights over the south-western slopes of the mountains," she said. Now she was looking at him straightly, and the fork rested lightly in her hand. "My father had leased them from the Nhovis for forty years. He used to rent out claims to any prospectors who wanted to try their luck. If anyone struck gold or silver, and there was nothing else worth mining, he used to get a small percentage of the yield. The Nhovis had half of the rest. That was all. And he had an agreement with every prospector that if they struck it rich, he would have a larger share."

"And you sold the lease."

"Yes."

"For ten thousand dollars."

"For ten thousand dollars," she repeated.

"Why?"

"I wanted to leave Red Rock. I didn't think I could ever live there again. And I didn't want anything to do with working the gold. At the time, it seemed as if the gold had really killed my father." After a moment, Judith said stonily: "Simon, this food will get cold if——"

"Listen to me, Judy. Why did you sell out? Why were you so anxious to get away from Red Rock? You love the country, you're part of it, you've eaten your heart out ever since you left. What drove you away?"

"Si——"

"*What drove you away?*"

She didn't answer. He could tell by the movement of her shoulders as she turned her back on him, that she was crying, or fighting against tears. Simon stood up slowly. He went nearer to her but did not touch her.

"Judy, what drove you away?" he demanded again, and when she didn't answer, he went on: "Do you fear that Laughing Water Smith killed your father? Did *he* undermine the rock so that it fell? Is that what you really fear?" And when she did not answer again, he went on in a harsher voice: "Did he set the trap at the cave? Is that what you think, Judy? You've got to tell me!"

Chapter 18

SURROUNDED

Judith stood so still that it was almost as if she had stopped breathing. The sizzling of fat on the dishes faded and silence fell again. The shadows of the mountain peaks were striking out towards them like dark spears of menace.

"Judith——"

She turned round, taking her hands away from her face; there were tears in her eyes and on her cheeks.

"No," she said, "I left because I felt that I hated Red Rock country for what it had done to my father. And I left because Morrell was in possession, and he seemed to think that the lease included me."

"You?" Simon asked sharply.

"He wanted me to go and live with him," Judith answered. "He wouldn't stop pestering me. With that on top of everything else, I couldn't stay. But—but that isn't important, now. Simon, listen to me. Only Laughing Water knew that if his hat was outside the cave, it was an 'all clear' signal." She caught her breath. "I can't believe it means what it seems to mean, but——"

Simon said unemotionally: "Did you suspect Laughing Water in New York?"

"No," she said. "I didn't, and yet——" She drew a step nearer. "I didn't believe my father would die in an ordinary rock fall. I believed someone had caused the rock to fall, by undermining it, perhaps with an explosion. It had to be someone who knew the mountains well, but I couldn't even think of Laughing Water—I tell you I didn't even *think* of him. I thought it was Morrell, or someone whom Morrell paid." She turned towards the fire and sank down, wearily. "It wasn't until I saw his hat and the trap, that I began to go over it again. If it was Laughing Water, then he was ready to kill me as well as my father."

"Yet—Morrell sent Gatz and the others after us."

"No one could be sure where we would come," Judith said. She took a torn handkerchief from her pocket and dabbed at her eyes. "This bacon will be congealed, you'll hate it!" She gave a tense, hurt smile. "Shall I warm it up? It'll be three hours before we get to the next hiding place."

"We'll eat it as it is," Simon said. They ate in silence for a few minutes, then he said quietly: "Is that all you're frightened of?"

"Why yes, what else could there be?"

"Judy."

"Si, don't——"

"Judy, can you think of any other reason why Laughing Water Smith should murder your father?" When she didn't answer, he went on: "We've assumed that if he did, he did it for money, that he was paid to. Was there any other cause for hatred between them?"

"I don't know of any," she answered. "They were always such good friends. Simon, I've told you everything I know. I can't go on talking about it, I just can't go on."

He did not believe her, but felt sure that she was holding something back—that she might even be lying. He hated the thought of that, but the conviction grew strong and compelling—and with it came understanding of the gravity of the expression in her eyes, the curious silences, the way she had turned away from him, the way she had looked past him—not simply into the distance or the past, but because she could not meet his gaze. He felt quite sure that he was right—but to force the issue now might drive her into a stubborn silence. He would try to make her talk more freely, later.

"All right," he said. "All right, Judy." He took the coffee pot off the fire, poured out, and stirred in sugar with a paper spoon. Then he stood up.

In the tension of the past twenty minutes he had hardly been aware of the change in the light, but now night was falling fast. He finished his coffee, and without a word they packed up and started off. Obviously, Judith knew where to go, and did not even look at the sky, where the brighter stars were beginning to stand out.

110

The next stage in the journey should take three hours, she told him, but it might take longer in the darkness.

She had not warned him of difficult climbing, but as they went on the mesa seemed to become rougher. There was hardly enough light for them to see the bigger rocks, and get round them.

"I feel as if I'm walking towards the edge of the world," Judith said, quite suddenly.

He knew exactly what she meant, and there was no need for comment. Yet in the silence between them, his conviction that she was hiding some truth from him grew and grew, and became a shadow between them.

*   *   *

"We're nearly there," she said at last.

"How far?"

"Perhaps another five minutes," Judith said. She put a hand on his arm to halt him. "Listen."

They stood perfectly still, while through the empty silence there came to them the distant sound of splashing water.

"It's the only water near," she told him. "There's a ravine which starts up in the higher mountains, and the snow melts and comes this way—it's only a trickle, now, and in a month's time it will be dried up completely."

"Does Laughing Water camp by it?"

"No," she said. "That would be too obvious. He has another cave, facing the waterfall."

When she stopped they could hear the splashing more clearly, and it forced its way into Simon's consciousness like the ceaseless ticking of a clock. They went on, feeling their way.

"Were all his camping places hiding places?" Simon asked.

"I don't understand you."

"Are all the places where Laughing Water Smith kept stores and emergency rations hidden away like these?"

"Yes."

"But he shared them with you and your father."

"Yes," she said; and after a pause, went on: "Be careful here, there's a kind of natural staircase in the hillside. I'll lead the way."

"He shared secret hiding places just with you and your father," Simon said. "Why were they so secret?"

"Because other hunters and prospectors might have raided them."

111

Simon said: "Would they? Wouldn't they always come well-provisioned?"

"Simon, we mustn't talk here. There might be another trap."

"Wouldn't all hunters be as anxious to keep emergency supplies in different places over the mountains in case they got into difficulties?" he insisted.

"Be very careful here," she said.

"I'm being careful. Answer me, Judy. Isn't that true?"

He saw her lower herself over the lip of a ledge, followed, and for at least three minutes climbed down backwards, groping step by step. Then they came to level ground again, and Simon asked stubbornly:

"Isn't it true, Judy?"

"Yes," she said. "Si——"

"What don't you want to believe?" demanded Simon, roughly. "Your father and Laughing Water built these caches all about the mountains and made them as inaccessible and secret as possible. Hunters would not do that. Prospectors might do if they'd made a strike, but they would only want to hide a strike from other people, they wouldn't want to hide food and emergency supplies. Why did Laughing Water and your father hide so much?"

She spun round on him.

"*What are you trying to say about my father?*"

"Judy," he said, "I'm not trying to say anything about him or anyone. I'm trying to sort out the truth. There is a reason for all this—a reason for his death, a reason for what happened to me twenty-five years ago, a reason for the fact that the steward Marchesi killed my aunt and was killed himself, a reason why we've been in danger since I set foot in Red Rock. Judy, listen to me. You went to see Laughing Water, he wasn't there, but he would be sure that you would start out to look for him. Wouldn't he?"

She didn't answer.

"*Wouldn't he?*"

"Yes," she admitted, in a low-pitched voice. "Yes, he would, but——"

She stopped. For a moment he thought that she was still fighting this battle of deception with herself, that the idolised, idealised figures of her childhood and of her life were too fragile and too delicate, and the thought of damaging them hurt her. But he sensed something different, now. He heard her sharp intake of breath and saw her turn her head.

"Was your father plotting to steal from the others? Were

112

Smith and Morrell and your father working together? *Did thieves fall out?* Is that why you couldn't stay in Red Rock country?"

"Quiet!" Judith breathed.

For a moment he thought she was simply trying to stop him. Then he sensed that she was listening intently. His heart began to pound. He felt her hand against his arm, and they stood close together, peering into the near darkness. The monotonous splash of the waterfall sounded even more clearly, like the tick of an infernal machine, and he hated it; but then he heard a different sound. Footsteps? His heart was thudding now, and there was a suffocating pressure at his throat.

A man coughed.

Judith whispered: "They're here!"

"Perhaps only one," Simon murmured.

The faint cough was repeated; then a sound to the left, and another above them. They were surrounded by enemies.

Why didn't they close in?

It was as if they had known all along that their quarry would come here. Of what use was his rifle, now? He could not shoot at darkness.

Then Judith made a sound, as of a bird whistling—and from some distance off there came an echo of the sound. As it came, she moved away from him; and as she moved, a flashlight shone out on her face, and another shone on his.

A man said: "So you've brought him, Judy."

After a pause, and before the crushing significance of the words came to Simon, Judith said in a flat voice:

"Yes, I've brought him."

Chapter 19

DELILAH

Judith's words came in a low-pitched voice, but they seemed to echo and re-echo about the hidden valley. The light shone stark on her pale face, and the hard brilliance of her eyes.

"*Yes, I've brought him.*"

Another light shone out, stabbing the ground close to Simon's feet, rising sharply on to ugly rocks, then catching the butt of the rifle.

The man who had spoken said: "Throw down your gun, Coll."

Simon didn't move.

"Three revolvers are trained on you," the speaker said. "Throw the rifle down."

Simon did not move.

The man said: "Al," as simply as that. There was a click of sound, followed by the sharp bark of a shot reverberating about the valley, shattering against Simon's ears. The bullet struck the earth a few inches from his feet, and broken rock sprayed over his legs.

"Just throw down that rifle," the man ordered again.

Simon was trying to fight through the black despair which Judith's words had brought; trying to control his voice, his body, his mind. He wanted to struggle, to shoot, to shout—but reason held him back. If he were covered, then before he could raise the rifle to shoot he himself would be shot dead, for he knew that at least three men were here.

"I'll tell you again," the unseen man said. "Just once."

Simon put his hand to his shoulder, hooking the strap of the rifle high. He eased it over his arm, and let it fall. Every moment seemed to increase the tension of the watching men and the brightness of the light on his face; he thought there was an easing of that tension as the rifle clattered to the ground. The flashlight which shone on Judith was switched off; Simon was now the only visible one among them—watched by those invisible eyes. The torch did not waver. The ordeal by light seemed unending, and as he stood there he began to wonder why it was kept on so long; it was as if someone were scrutinising him feature by feature.

Suddenly the light went out.

"So that's him," a man said. "I wanted to see you, Coll, when I knew you'd got this far. I wanted to make sure Marchesi was right."

Simon didn't speak.

"He was dead right," Morrell went on. "He saw you when you were with your aunt, a year ago—and he took a picture. When I saw it I realised that Laughing Water had a son. You're the image of your father when he was young, Simon Coll. You have to look hard to see the resemblance now, but you are the image of him when he was younger."

Simon caught his breath.

"I didn't lose any time finding out if Martha Tenby had tol‹

114

you who you were," Morrell said. "You want to know something? She wrote a letter to Laughing Water, but I intercepted it, and I discovered all about his precious son. I knew then that I had to do plenty. I saw Martha in Weymouth in February this year, and she said that nothing would stop her from telling you the truth. But something did, didn't it?"

Simon said: "I'll find a way to kill you."

"Not in a million years," sneered Morrell.

Judith said: "Simon, I——"

"Just don't talk to me," Simon said roughly. "Don't talk to me." There was bitter anger in his voice. "Keep right away from me."

The man in front of him laughed, a mocking sound in the darkness.

"He doesn't seem to like you any more, Judy—he's a man of very strong emotions." There was a pause, a long, hanging pause, and then went on: "Like his father."

Simon clamped his teeth together.

"Just like his father," the unseen man went on. "Okay, Al, get him and let's go."

There was a scuffling of footsteps and men loomed up in front of Simon; two of them clutched his arms. Flashlights shone out, their beams more diffused, showing the serried natural ledges in steps which led down the side of the valley. The splashing of the water seemed louder, and once Simon caught sight of a silvery streak as water fell. It was fairly easy to climb down. He saw a platform with a stone wall as protection from the steep drop into the depth of the valley. A man stood by it, and there was a light close to it—dim and eerie. It shone on Judith. Simon reached the platform, and hesitated; one man's grip on his arm tightened, and he was forced to turn round.

He saw a tunnel.

It was high enough for him to stand upright. Tall wooden props supported it. At intervals of twenty feet or so along the tunnel a dim light glowed. One of the men went ahead, one followed him, and Simon, walking between them, had no chance of turning round, no chance of escape. He saw stalactic formations, and his mind flashed back to trips he had made to the caves at Cheddar Gorge; but this cave seemed to dwarf not only the Somerset caves but the whole of the gorge itself. He had a sensation of vastness as he stared ahead. The moving figure near the light seemed unreal—but that feeling vanished when he saw the big man standing by a table made of rough hewn wood. Judith was standing by the end of the table, but Simon did not look at her. He looked at the face of Lewis Morrell. Undoubtedly this was the man who had stepped into the black Cadillac. The hooded eyes, the big features, the prominent nose, the full lips—there was no mistaking the man.

"Bring him nearer," Morrell ordered.

There were at least a dozen men in the cave, and yet they were lost in its vastness.

"Where's the old man?"

"Waiting," someone said with a ghost of a chuckle.

"Bring him here," Morrell ordered, and looked into Simon's face. "You've come a long way to see your father, Coll. I guess I won't deny you that as you've got so far."

There was a rustle of movement, and then a man was thrust out of the darkness towards the light—a tall, elderly man, with clear, sharp features, a face so like the face of the man whom Simon had always imagined as Laughing Water Smith that it was like looking at a fantasy which had come to life. Simon felt an icy coldness in his veins, a great sense of shock, although he had been keyed up for this since Morrell had talked of his father.

The man's eyes were clear and bright. There was fearlessness in them, and he stood erect and proud, as if indifferent to those about him. Near the edge of the shadowy darkness Judy was standing, arms limp by her side.

"Take off that gag," Morrell ordered. "He can't do any harm now."

As the gag fell, Laughing Water moistened his lips and tried to speak, but his mouth was stiff and parched, and he could make no sound.

A man said: "So they're here, so we've got what we had to have, Lew. What are we waiting for?"

"We aren't waiting for a thing," Morrell answered, without looking round. "We'll be here until sun-up, and if they're dead when we leave, that's in good time." He turned to Judith, and there was an unmistakable softening in his voice as he went on: "I didn't think you would do it, Judy. I didn't trust you. Why did you?"

She didn't speak.

"I don't believe it was just the money," Morrell said. "When I paid Albert Wegel fifty thousand dollars to stop bothering me, and offered you twenty-five thousand to bring Coll here, Wegel said you wouldn't do it for a million dollars. Why did you, Judy?" There was a mocking note in his voice. "You don't mean to tell me that you love me after all." She didn't answer. "Is that the answer?" Morrell demanded. "Do you love me, Judy?"

"No," she said stonily. "I hate you, as I have always done, and all you stand for."

"But you brought Coll," Morrell reminded her.

"I had to bring him here," she said. "I had to bring him to see his father." She raised her eyes towards Simon, and went on in a voice so low-pitched that he could hardly hear her. "Simon, I knew that we hadn't a chance. I knew Morrell and the others would kill us in New York, or on the way here, or somewhere in the Red Mountains. There never was a real chance for us. And you had to see your father." She looked from him to Morrell, and went on scathingly: "Do you think I would trust you as far as the nearest gun-hand?" she demanded. "You wouldn't have paid me twenty-five thousand dollars. You wanted to get me here and kill me in another accident. Money wouldn't have brought me here, only a fool would think it might."

Morrell said: "I don't fool easily, honey, and the sure fact is I brought you here." He was smiling crookedly at her; there was a rough handsomeness in his face and a rough strength in his manner. "But you don't have to die, Judy. They have to die, but you need not. You can string along with me for as long as you like, and you won't go short of a thing. I always told you, I like a woman with plenty of spirit, in and out of bed. Don't get a heroine complex, Judy—heroines can be an awful bore."

"Can they?" she said, heavily. She closed her eyes for a moment, and then looked at Simon. "Simon," she said, "I could have told you, but if you'd known you would never have trusted me. I tried to get to Laughing Water first, but when I saw that hat, at the cave, and that booby trap, I knew he was a prisoner, and the only way for you was to bring you here.

"I could have warned you, but—we could never have escaped. You wouldn't have got this far on your own. I thought it better to bring you here to see your father, than to let you die without any knowledge of him.

"But if I'd told you, Simon, you wouldn't have come, you would have tried to escape over the mountains, and I knew there was no hope of that." She pressed a hand against her forehead. "Si," she went on, "you've got to believe me."

After a long pause, Morrell jeered:

"Sure, he believes you. Just look at his face."

"Si," Judith said, "you've got to believe me."

*　　*　　*

117

The dark emptiness of the cave seemed to press down upon Simon, shutting in the grin on Morrell's face, with its story of overwhelming self confidence; the tall man, his father, proud and unafraid; and Judith.

* * *

"Simon," Judy said again, and he could only just hear her voice, "you've got to believe me." She was staring at him through the semi-darkness; he could see the flash of her eyes and hear the passionate pleading in her voice. "It was the only way I could make sure you found him, and the only way he could find you." She turned to Morrell. He was grinning with that look of mockery but something in her expression drove the grin away. "You tried to make sure they could never meet," she said. "You've kept them apart for twenty-five years. Let them have time to talk now— give them a little time."

"For what?" a man jeered.

"It won't do any harm," she pleaded. "There's nothing any of us can do now." She looked towards the pale light of the tunnel which led from the entrance, and drew a deep breath. "I know you'll never let us out of here. At least give us a few hours together."

"I told you, honey, you can be as free as the air," Morrell said.

"And I've told you, nothing will make me live with you."

"Won't it?" asked Morrell, and he took a step forward. For a moment it looked as if he would seize hold of her, and her hands went up, to fend him off. He stopped just short of her, and went on roughly: "You and Coll and Laughing Water can talk for as long as you like—on just one condition."

"What condition?"

"You come with me in the morning," he said. "You come with me, and you stay for as long as I want you. You can please yourself whether you live with me or die here." He made a brief sign to the man behind him, who grabbed Simon's arms and held him back. "But if you prefer to die, we'll get it over with, right now."

The man named Al whispered: "Now you're talking."

Chapter 20

THE WORDS OF LAUGHING WATER

Judith did not try to move away. Simon made a quick move forward, but his guard poked a gun in his back, and swore at him, viciously; it was the only sound except for their breathing.

She could live or die.

If robbing him and Laughing Water of a few hours of life would save her, he would gladly kill himself. But there was so much more. Her whole future. He could picture it; a few years with Morrell, a few years as a rich man's mistress, hating it but becoming inured—and in the years afterwards, a chance of contentment and happiness? It could be so. What did he want her to do? Would it make any difference if he told her now? Would she listen—would she even hear him? She was staring into Morrell's face, as if the man had cast a spell over her, robbing her of speech.

Nothing else mattered; not even the answer to the questions which had seemed so urgent not long ago—why had he been left in England, why had Morrell meant to keep him in ignorance of his identity? These questions hovered dimly in the back of his mind.

What would Judith do?

Then he heard Laughing Water speaking. The voice was husky, as if it had not been used for a long time, his expression serene, yet touched with authority.

"The young are not meant to die, Judy," he said. "For my son and for me there is only the night left, but you can have tomorrow." As he spoke, he began to smile. "Don't throw life away. It wasn't given to you to throw away."

There was deathly silence.

"Judy——" Simon began.

"Be quiet, son," Laughing Water said. "Don't make it any harder for her than it has to be."

"I can hardly believe it," said Morrell, jeering. "Sense, at last. That's good advice, honey, very good advice. I'll let him talk you into it." He turned away. "Put them in that inner cave," he said. "They can't get away from there."

"Lew, I tell you——" Al began.

"Do what I tell you," Lewis Morrell said. "You haven't any

stake in this. I've a big one." He turned to look at Judy, and Simon had a strange impression: that in spite of his brutality, his mocking, his jeering, Judith meant a great deal to him. He himself did not know what to think, could not begin to think. Laughing Water might be right, but in the vivid imagery with which he had lived for so long, Simon could picture Judith's slim body crushed against Morrell's, and he hated the picture; but he would not be alive to know about it.

"The young are not meant to die," Laughing Water had said. Laughing Water—his own father.

The man Al moved towards them, gun in hand, and two others came to hustle them into the inner cave.

It was cold and dimly lit, the only couch the hard ground, the only sound their breathing.

*　　*　　*

"Listen to me, my son," said Laughing Water. "You must persuade Judith to do what Morrell wants, and you must let him hear you telling her." He spoke in a whisper which hardly reached Simon's ears. "In a few minutes, in half-an-hour perhaps, you can shout that at her, make it sound as if you're quarrelling. You have to leave her here, with me, and go and plead with Morrell for your life. Do you hear and understand me?"

"I can hear you," Simon said.

He could not understand any part of these extraordinary events. He was more confused than he had been since he had discovered that Judith had led him here. There was so much he wanted to know, so much.

"You hear but you do not understand," Laughing Water said. "Listen carefully, my son. The fifth lamp from the tunnel, by the white pillar, gives no light. In the rock near this is a small hole, and in the hole a stick of dynamite with a contact detonator. I have used this kind for blasting very often, and when I realised the danger here, I put that stick in position. Take it firmly, stand behind the pillar, and throw it towards the entrance. Crouch low, or you will be killed with the blast. When it is over, come back to us. There is a way of escape which Morrell does not know about.'

It was like the opening of a locked door.

"Can you be sure?" Simon asked.

"No, not sure," said Laughing Water. "But there is a reasonable chance that the explosion will close the entrance which the use. Some of them will be killed, a few will be left outside, other will be buried in here, but there are sufficient supplies for them until the police can come and dig them out." He paused and his hand touched Simon's. "The police will come with State Troopers even if only one of us escapes and sends for them. If we cannot escape, then no one can." It was almost impossible to see his lips moving as he spoke, and fierce excitement set Simon's blood pulsing. He found himself crushing Judith's hand.

"Judy can do this thing," Laughing Water said, "or you can, my son."

"I want an answer to one question," Simon said. "When I throw the dynamite, why can't you make sure that you two are safe?"

"If we come outside we shall suffer from the explosion, and if we hide in here—as we must—the entrance might be blocked," the old man answered simply. "If it is only loosely blocked you will be able to help us out. You will be the only conscious man in the cave—provided just one thing happens."

He broke off.

"What thing?" demanded Simon, hoarsely.

"Provided the explosion does not bring down the roof. There is no way of telling what will happen once the mouth of the cave is blocked." There was a long pause before he went on: "Is it true —Martha Tenby is dead?"

Simon said: "Yes, she's dead."

Now it was hard to make himself remember Aunt Martha, or to think of anything but the fifth lamp near the white pillar. He could remember that pillar, a thick and massive stalagmite, likely to withstand almost any blast, perfectly placed for Laughing Water's purpose. He did not need to ask why the old man had planned all this; he could see that Laughing Water and Judith had worked together to bring about this situation and there was nothing surprising in the plan—all he wanted was to go outside, get to that dynamite, and throw it as far from the white pillar as he could.

"She was a very good woman, Martha Tenby," said Laughing Water. "Did she ever tell you about yourself?"

Simon said: "No."

"She promised that she would not do so. She thought it better that you should never know unless I could come to claim you," Laughing Water said, "and I believe she was right, my son. Your mother was a young woman of a good family. When we met, we fell in love, meeting in secret in the place that gave you your name."

121

Simon waited in a stillness which almost seemed to choke him.

"We wanted to marry, but she was too young by English law, and I needed permission from my Commanding Officer which I knew would not be given quickly. The ship was due to sail for manoeuvres and I did not know when it would come back, so I swore that I was British and your mother claimed to be older than she was. We made false declarations, because we wanted to give you a name."

Laughing Water closed his eyes as if the memory hurt him, and it was a long time before he went on:

"But the ship did come back soon, and your mother and I knew much happiness—until she fell gravely ill. I had to be with her, but my ship was under orders to sail again, this time for the Pacific. God knows what would have happened had I told the Commanding Officer the truth, but I was far too frightened. I deserted my ship, and went to your mother. We hired a caravan, on a hill overlooking Weymouth bay. You were born there as your mother died. I was left with you—and with one friend, your mother's sister Martha, whom we told when it was too late.

"And Martha said that she would take you, and bring you up as her own."

Judith's hand slid into Simon's.

"I left you on the Coll, and Martha came for you," Laughing Water went on. "I sent all the money I had to a lawyer friend of hers, and then tried to find a merchant ship. But I was recognised, and taken back to the navy. I hardly cared. I was grief-stricken and very bitter, and all I wanted was to forget. I said nothing about my marriage or about you. My punishment was not severe, so I returned to my own people as soon as I was free. A young officer who befriended me knew Red Rock country, and knew that I was the chief of the Nhovi Indians, owners of much land and the mineral rights to it. Later I learned that he believed there was a big gold lode in the mountains, and he knew that uranium ore was already being mined.

"He was Morrell.

"He took over many mining rights nearby, he bought land, he squeezed out smaller miners, he used our friendship to help him. I began to realise what kind of man he was, but he had befriended me at a time of great trouble, and I could not forget that debt.

"I had told him of my marriage, but not that I had a son. Then about a year ago, I wrote to Martha Tenby. She replied at once but I did not get the letter. Ma Neilson, knowing of Morrell' interest in me, gave it to him. It caused Martha Tenby's death," Laughing Water went on, "and soon I knew that it might cause yours. Already I was in great danger, partly because I knew Judy's father had been murdered, partly because I was last in line of Nhovi royal blood to be able to claim the mineral rights to Red Rock country. I could prove that Morrell had killed my friend but if I stood against Morrell there was much more than my past, much more than gold, at stake. There was Judith's life. I dared not risk it."

Laughing Water paused, and then went on: "I am the sole surviving chief of the Nhovi Indians, who once lived and thrived in the Red Mountains. Now, there are but a few of that tribe left, and it would be quite easy for Morrell to drive them out, as he owns the land. I had to do everything I could to save them. While Judith's father was alive there was no difficulty. He owned the leases in the mountains, he allowed all Nhovis a share of all the strikes, he was good and understanding. But this man Morrell— he is a killer, by nature. While he lives, there will be no good in these mountains. Until tonight, I did not think there would be any hope of defeating him, but when I heard that you were coming I left the cabin. I was followed all the time by Morrell's men, but came in through a deep hole in another part of this cave. I came when Morrell's men were camped outside. I put the explosive by that lamp—explosive powerful enough to do all we require.

"Then I had to lure Morrell inside here, after you and Judith.

"Because you are my son, and my son inherits all of the Nhovi land still owned by this tribe. But part of that land is needed by Morrell. He could silence me because of Judith, but he could not silence you, he could only kill you.

"Now do you see, my son?"

Chapter 21

THE INHERITANCE

The silence was profound; even the men outside had stopped moving about and talking. Simon felt Judith's hand on his again, and he drew her to him, and slid his arm about her.

"Simon," she whispered, "I had to bring you."

"If you'd only told me——" he began, and realised how impossible it would have been for her to be sure that he would have come with her. But that hardly mattered. The past and the future hinged on the present; there was no time to savour the news of the past and it was only folly to look into the future.

"Yes, Laughing Water," he said, "I see and understand everything you've done. The plan is a good one." He gripped Judith's arm fiercely as he went on: "It's time I went out, it's time we started to quarrel. They'll probably think I'm mad!" He groped for and found Laughing Water's hand and felt the pressure of the bony fingers; then he went on in a sharp, angry voice: "But they've got to let me go. They've got to. I don't care what I do. I don't want to die any more than Judith does. They've got to let me go!"

*　　*　　*

The lights outside were all on, except the fifth near the white pillar.

Morrell, the man Al and two others were sitting in canvas chairs round a small table, laden with dirty plates. As Simon appeared, Morrell grinned. Al dropped his hand to his revolver. There were two men between Simon and that fifth lamp, and he did not yet know how he would be able to reach it; he only knew that he must.

"Morrell, there's no need to talk about killing me," he said. "I can't help what happens to Laughing Water. I'll work with you—on your own terms, of course."

"So the guy ain't no hero," Al sneered.

"It doesn't sound like it," said Lewis Morrell. "What's the trouble, Coll? Are you disappointed in your old man now you've found him?"

Simon said: "Listen, Morrell, I came out here to find my father, that's natural enough isn't it? Then I fell in love with Judy and wanted to help her, but—*who wants to die*?"

"Coll," Morrell sneered, "you certainly don't."

"Of course I don't, and—listen! Judy will see it your way, I'm sure she will. Morrell—give me a chance, let me prove how useful I can be to you."

Morrell stood staring at him.

Al said: "No, he's no hero. He's just a rat."

"He's the rat who shot four of our boys this morning," Morrell said. "He had guts then. What's the real trouble, Coll? The truth about your father?"

124

Simon said savagely: "What difference does it make? I've never seen him before in my life. I wish to God I never had!" He closed his eyes, went forward, dropping his voice as if trying to make sure that only Morrell heard what he said next. "Listen, Mr. Morrell, the old man's got something up his sleeve. It's over here. If I tell you what it is, will you give me a chance?"

"So the old devil had something up his sleeve," Morrell said, softly. "Who's surprised? What is it, Coll?"

"I'll show you if——"

Morrell slapped him across the face with sudden fury, slapped him again, and made him stagger back; and now he was much closer to the white pillar, it was within a few yards of him.

"I asked you what it is," said Morrell. "Now tell me or you'll know what it is to get hurt."

"It—it's another way out," Simon muttered. His cheeks were flaming and his jaws ached from the force of the blows, but he fought back the impulse to fling himself bodily at this man. "I'll show you how to get to it." He backed away, as if afraid that Morrell would strike him again. "This way," he muttered, gasping between each word. "Just past the white pillar, just big enough for a man to crawl through."

Morrell said: "Al, go and check."

Al nodded, and walked past. Simon felt the cold glass of the lamp bulb against the back of his hand. He saw the shallow hole beyond; and the dynamite. He picked up the explosive, as if touching the wall to keep his balance, and neither Morrell nor the man with him showed any suspicion.

Morrell and the others were further out in the cave; Al was close to the wall. Simon tossed the stick towards the tunnel and the entrance, and jumped back behind the pillar. He saw Morrell snatch at his pocket, as if for a gun, felt a sharp bite of pain followed by the roar of a shot—and then the explosion came, with a flash of blinding light. He pitched face downwards behind the pillar, gasping for breath, covering his head with his arms. Small pieces of rock began to fall from the roof, and he heard the rumbling of a heavier fall further along the cave. Dust choked him, and he dared not uncover his face. Gradually, silence settled. When at last he looked up he saw a great jagged hole in the ceiling. He struggled to his feet, and staggered towards the inner cave where he had left Laughing Water and Judith.

No one else moved.

* * *

The climb to the back of the cave took them nearly two hours.

Then there was a long haul with a dangling rope to help drag themselves up. The escape route was like a natural chimney in the rocks, and it seemed to go on for ever; but the time came when the stars shone down on them.

*　　*　　*

Simon looked at Judith, without a word.

"We can rest here for the night, and then go to one of the other hiding places, where a Nhovi will take a message to the State Police at Flagstaff," Laughing Water was saying. "With all three of us as witnesses, there will be no escape now for Morrell. Even if we cannot prove that he murdered your father, Judith, for his leases, we can prove many other crimes against him."

"We'll get those leases back," Simon said.

*　　*　　*

Three months later, after the arrest, the trials, and Morrell's execution with those of three of his men, the final court judgments came through. The land was returned to its original lease owners; the sale to Morrell was proved to be null and void.

The news came almost as an anti-climax, as Simon and Judith stood at the entrance to the cabin built not far from Laughing Water's in the foothills of the Red Mountains. The cliffs were as vivid and as powerful as ever, but the angry threat had gone from them.

The Nhovi Indians came and went at will, and mined the gold, taking their share. Prospectors came and staked claims and were given all they needed. Ma Neilson had left for the west coast, and Andy Lapp now managed the café, the cabins and the gas station.

The sun shone benignly on the log roof of the new cabin, on Simon and his wife Judith, on Laughing Water now living happily higher up in the foothills. There were letters tucked into the little metal box as the days went on; congratulations from Lessinger, from old Taggart, from the Fraills, from Dorothy. There was a letter from the Geness family on Long Island. There was even a mention in Albert Wegel's column, telling the world that the honeymoon was being spent in the beauty and the grandeur of the foothills, now freed from fear.

THE END